The Great Reindeer DISASTER

Kate Saunders

ILLUSTRATED BY NEAL LAYTON

90 YEARS OF EXCELLENCE
FABER & FABER

About the author

KATE SAUNDERS is a full-time author and journalist. Her books for children have won awards and received rave reviews, and include future classics such as *Beswitched*, *Magicalamity*, *The Whizz Pop Chocolate Shop*, *The Curse of the Chocolate Phoenix*, Carnegie shortlisted *The Land of Neverendings* and Costa Winner *Five Children on the Western Front*. Kate lives in London.

About the illustrator

NEAL LAYTON was born and raised in Chichester. Whilst he was growing up he spent much of his time playing in the dirt, making homemade catapults and drawing pictures. He studied BA Graphic Design at Newcastle, and MA Illustration at Central Saint Martins. Neal now lives in Portsmouth with his family.

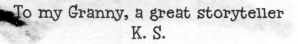

To my Granny, a great storyteller
K. S.

For Arabelle and Hunter
N. L.

First published in 2019
by Faber & Faber Limited
Bloomsbury House,
74–77 Great Russell Street,
London WC1B 3DA

Printed by CPI Group (UK) Ltd, Croydon CR0 4YY

A CIP record for this book
is available from the British Library

ISBN 978-0-571-34898-5

FSC
www.fsc.org
MIX
Paper from
responsible sources
FSC® C020471

2 4 6 8 10 9 7 5 3 1

ONE
A Holiday Surprise

It started as a normal family holiday. The Trubshaws were in Devon, staying in a lovely cottage that was right on the beach.

Mr David Trubshaw was short and rather fat and worked with computers. Mrs Judy Trubshaw was tall and thin with long blonde hair, and she was a part-time librarian. They had two children – Jake, aged ten, and seven-year-old Sadie. Jake thought his little sister

The Trubshaws

was incredibly bossy and always bursting into tears to get her own way, and Sadie thought her brother boasted too much about being the oldest, but otherwise they got on pretty well. And they both loved the seaside.

It was the end of July and the weather was so boiling hot that Mum spent the first day covering Jake and Sadie with gloopy sunblock. Lunch was a delicious beach picnic of tomatoes and ice cream. In the afternoon, Sadie dug a deep hole in the sand and Jake splashed in the sea. The waves were perfect – big enough to be fun, but not big enough to be dangerous. Sadie only cried once, when some sunblock accidentally got into her mouth. In the evening they had a fabulous supper of fish and chips, and went to bed.

That was the first day of the holiday.

And also the last.

* * *

In the middle of the night, when the Trubshaws were all fast asleep and the only sound was the steady swishing of the waves on the beach, something suddenly smashed into the roof of the cottage with such a gigantic **THUMP** that the whole place shook and they all woke up. Sadie started to cry. Dad turned on the light and put on his glasses.

'David, go out and look!' squeaked Mum, hugging Sadie. 'Something's fallen on the roof – see what it is!'

'I'll look,' said Jake, grabbing his cricket bat in case he needed a weapon.

The noises began again – violent scrapings and scrabblings that seemed to come from inside the walls.

'Do calm down, everybody,' said Dad. 'Some silly animal has got itself trapped in the chimney, that's all.'

Sadie stopped crying and said, 'Poor thing, it must be frightened.'

'We should set it free,' said Jake. 'It must be stuck.'

They all went downstairs to the sitting room of the cottage, where there was an old-fashioned fireplace so big that the children could stand up in it. The scrabbling and scraping was louder down here, and old soot rained down into the empty grate.

'Well,' said Dad, 'if that's a mouse, it's a very big one.'

There was a single moment of stillness and silence – and then the Trubshaw family heard something very strange indeed.

'UGH! UGH!' spluttered a voice in the chimney. 'UGH . . . oh NO! Oh HELP!'

There was a series of rapid thumps, and whoever (or whatever) was up the chimney shouted,

'OUCH . . .
        OOF . . .
                BUM . . .
                        BUM . . .
                                BUM!' and landed in a great whoosh of soot that made them all cough.

It was the most amazing thing any of them had ever seen. The creature in the fireplace was the size of a very large dog or a very small cow, but it had antlers and little hooves.

'I think that's a reindeer,' said Mum faintly. 'But what's a reindeer doing in Devon?'

They all stared as the tubby little reindeer stepped out of the fireplace. 'Hello,' it said breathlessly. 'Sorry about that.'

'Good grief,' muttered Dad. 'This doesn't feel like a dream, but I must be dreaming – reindeer can't talk!'

Jake and Sadie were the first to recover. While Mum and Dad gaped at their strange visitor like a pair of statues, they knelt down on the floor to look at it properly.

The reindeer stared at the children. The children stared at the reindeer.

'Is it safe to touch you?' asked Jake.

'Yes,' said the reindeer. 'I won't bite you or anything.'

They both reached out to stroke the light-brown fur on its back.

'My name's Sadie Trubshaw,' said Sadie. 'What's yours?'

'Percy,' said the reindeer in his growly voice. 'Percy Prancer.'

'I'm seven,' said Sadie. 'This is my brother Jake, who's ten. How old are you?'

'Oh . . . er . . .' For a few moments Percy's furry face looked shifty. 'Twenty-eight.'

'Really?' Jake was suspicious. 'Aren't you a bit small for a twenty-eight-year-old?'

'No,' said Percy. 'You obviously don't know much about reindeer.'

'How did you land on our roof?'

'I fell off the sleigh,' said Percy.

'What – you mean like Santa's sleigh?'

'Yes, of course,' said Percy. 'I'm a squadron leader in the Christmas Delivery Service. We were shooting presents on the Ireland run, and I fell off the sleigh when we hit a patch of bad weather.'

'But it's not Christmas!' cried Sadie. 'Why were you delivering Christmas presents in the middle of summer?'

'Well, it's complicated,' said Percy. 'Haven't you ever wondered how Father Christmas manages to deliver the whole world's presents in a single night?'

'He's magic,' said Sadie.

'He doesn't exist,' muttered Dad.

'David, don't be so silly,' said Mum. 'You're talking to a flying reindeer. I think it's fair to assume that Father Christmas is real.' She had got over being shocked, and she bent down to pat Percy's head. 'You're very dusty – did you hurt yourself?'

'I'm fine, thank you.' said Percy.

'Well, I need a cup of tea and a biscuit.' Mum stood up briskly. 'Would you like anything, Percy? I don't know what a reindeer eats.'

'Mince pies,' said Jake. 'He's a Christmas reindeer, don't forget.'

'And raw carrots,' said Sadie. 'Last Christmas I left a carrot beside my stocking and it was gone in the morning. Does that mean the reindeer really ate it?'

'Yes,' said Percy. 'Everyone in the Service appreciates the little treats that people leave out for the reindeer.'

'Oh, good,' said Mum. 'Would you like a cup of tea and a chocolate biscuit?'

'Yes please, Mrs Trubshaw.'

'Can you drink out of a cup, or would you rather have a bowl on the floor?'

'A bowl, please,' said Percy. 'With eight sugars.'

'What a polite little reindeer you are!' said Mum, smiling.

'Yuk – eight sugars!' said Jake.

Mum looked inside all the kitchen cupboards, but none of the bowls were big enough, so she made Percy's tea in Sadie's pink plastic bucket (she washed out the sand first) and put it down on the stone floor beside a chocolate biscuit on a plate. The polite reindeer trotted across the floor, his little hooves clicking, and stuck his head into the bucket.

'Oh, isn't he *sweet*?' cried Sadie.

'Can we keep him?' asked Jake. 'Can we take him home with us? Oh, please – I'll stop begging for a dog!'

'We should be helping Percy to get back to his own home,' said Mum, 'wherever that is.'

'The North Pole, of course,' said Sadie.

Percy finished his tea with a loud slurp and raised his head. 'The North Pole's just a docking point – I actually live on planet Yule-1.'

'**Wow, you come from another planet!**' said Jake. 'That makes you an alien and I've always wanted to meet a real alien.'

'Do you need to call anyone?' Mum held out her phone and looked doubtfully at Percy's hooves. 'I can do it for you, if you give me the number.'

'Thanks, Mrs Trubshaw, but I don't need to phone anybody,' said Percy. 'The microchip in my right antler has already been activated – all us reindeer are given microchips when we're born, in case we get lost during a delivery. They'll send down a transporter beam for me in a minute, so don't be shocked if I suddenly disappear.'

'Don't go yet!' said Sadie. 'You still haven't explained why you were delivering Christmas presents in summer.'

'It's such a huge job that it can only be done outside earth time,' said Percy. 'On planet Yule-1 every day is Christmas Eve and squadrons of flying reindeer deliver trillions of presents round the clock.'

'Now I know this is a dream, or a trick!' Dad said. He had got over the first shock, but was still refusing to believe his own eyes and ears. 'Microchips . . . transporter beams? This is *nonsense!*'

'No it's not,' said Sadie. 'It's magic.'

'But there's no such thing as– **OW!**'

The dark cottage was suddenly filled with a piercing white light that got stronger and stronger and made them all cover their eyes.

'That's my transporter beam,' said Percy. 'Goodbye and thank you for having me.'

Everything went pitch-dark, the cottage began to rock violently and the Trubshaws screamed with terror.

'What's happening?'
Mum gasped.
'Is it an earthquake?'
She grabbed Sadie and
Dad grabbed Jake.
A small, growly voice said,

'Whoops!'

And then the darkness
swallowed them.

TWO
The Truth About Percy

The next time the Trubshaws opened their eyes, they all gasped with shock and Sadie started to cry. Jake didn't cry, but he was very scared.

The cottage, the beach and the sea had vanished. They were strapped into seats in a windowless space that hummed and thrummed like an enormous tumble dryer.

'I don't remember getting on a plane,' said Mum.

'Where are we going?'

'We've been kidnapped,' said Jake.

'I want to go HOME!' wailed Sadie.

'OK, let's keep calm,' said Dad. 'There's bound to be a rational explanation.'

'I'm really, *really* sorry!' said a growly voice somewhere behind them. 'Oh crumbs – my mum's going to go mad!'

To everyone's surprise the small reindeer suddenly floated over their heads, his antlers scraping against the ceiling. He looked so funny with his little legs paddling in mid-air that Jake and Sadie stopped being scared and burst out laughing.

'Hello,' said Percy breathlessly. 'You haven't been kidnapped and you're not on a plane. I'm *really* sorry, but . . . well, the fact is that you got caught in my

transporter beam, and now you're in the space shuttle that's taking me back to my planet. Sorry!'

'We're in space!' said Jake. 'This is **BRILLIANT!**'

'I don't mind being in space if I'm with you,' said Sadie, beaming at Percy. 'Will we meet Rudolf? Does he really have a red nose?'

Jake unfastened his seat belt and floated gracefully out of his seat. 'Look at me – I'm weightless!' He turned a somersault in mid-air, and then did an upside-down dance on the ceiling that made Sadie and Percy shriek with laughter (Percy's laughing sounded like neighing). Sadie took off her own seat belt and all three of them had a hilarious time bumping against each other and walking up the walls.

'OK, that's enough,' said Dad. 'You two, get back in your seats and be quiet.' His round face was stern. 'I'd like a word with the squadron leader.'

He dragged the two children back into their seats, then he grabbed one of Percy's front legs and pulled the little reindeer down to eye level. 'You're not really a squadron leader, are you?'

'Not exactly,' said Percy, ducking his head so he wouldn't have to look at Dad. 'I might have exaggerated a bit.'

'I bet you're not twenty-eight, either,' said Jake. 'Or you wouldn't be worrying about your mum.'

'OK, I'm not exactly twenty-eight – but reindeer years are different to human years.'

'Come along, Percy!' Mum said kindly. 'It's time you told us the truth.'

'Don't be mean to him!' said Sadie. 'He's not lying . . . are you?'

Percy looked sulky for a moment, but then he sighed and said, 'I'm not a squadron leader. I'm not even in the Delivery Service, though I will be one day. This was all a terrible *mistake*! I wasn't supposed to be on that sleigh. Me and my friends were just having a look because it belongs to Wing Commander Dasher and the Jambusters and they're *legends*, but I got stuck in one of the gift chutes, and the sleigh took off before I could wriggle out of it.'

'Who are the Jambusters?' asked Sadie. 'Are they reindeer too?'

Percy's furry face was solemn. 'They're the most famous reindeer squadron, and the bravest – and the *coolest*! They got their name because they saved a whole town from a Christmas jam flood. Those daredevils laugh in the face of danger, and I'm going to join when I'm grown-up . . . I mean . . .' He realised what he had said and muttered, 'Oh, bum.'

'You might as well tell us your real age now,' said Mum.

Percy let out a long, neighing sigh. 'I'm nine.'

'Ha ha, I knew it!' cried Jake.

'I'm at primary school.'

'I'm glad you're not grown-up,' said Sadie. 'Now we can play with you. Is your school just for reindeer?'

'Reindeer and elves,' said Percy.

'**Elves!**' groaned Dad. 'This adventure is getting sillier by the minute! So elves are real, too?'

'Yes, Mr Trubshaw. One of my best friends is an elf.'

'Do you know how or why my family got sucked up by your transporter beam?'

'No, Mr Trubshaw.'

'I'm sure it wasn't your fault,' said Mum kindly. 'This is just a silly mix-up and we'll soon sort it out. Then we can go back to being on holiday.'

'I hope you're right,' said Dad. 'I booked that cottage for two weeks!'

There was a sharp **BLEEP**, a door swished open

in front of them and a voice said, 'Good evening, humans! My name is Captain Crisp. Space weather conditions are fine and we'll be landing on Yule-1 in half an hour.'

All the Trubshaws were struck into gaping silence, for they had never seen anyone like Captain Crisp. He was very small – about the same height as Sadie – and very obviously not human. His ears were enormous and slightly transparent, like the wings of a moth, and his skin was papery and wrinkled. He had a round head, a round body, very thin arms and legs and very big, bright-green eyes.

'I beg your pardon,' said Captain Crisp. 'I forgot that you humans have never seen my kind before. I'm an elf.'

'Of course you are,' muttered Dad. 'Silly me!'

'Excuse me,' said Mum. 'We're here by mistake and we need to get home to our own planet.'

'The authorities are aware of the situation, Mrs Trubshaw, and they're doing everything they can to put it right. Someone from the chairman's office will meet you at the docking point.' The captain's bug-like eyes flashed at Percy. 'And your mother will meet *you*.'

'**Uh-oh,**' said Percy. 'How cross is she – on a scale of one to ten?'

'Eleven,' said Captain Crisp. 'You're in a lot of trouble, young reindeer!'

* * *

Landing on planet Yule-1 was very strange and a little scary, but also exciting. The Trubshaws were locked into their seat belts and Percy was locked into his reindeer harness.

Captain Crisp's voice said, 'GRavity ON!' and suddenly everyone's body felt normal again.

'I've just realised,' said Mum, 'we're not dressed!' She was wearing a pink bathrobe and slippers, Dad was wearing his jeans and the baggy grey T-shirt he wore in bed, and Jake and Sadie were still in their pyjamas. 'If it's covered with snow we'll be freezing.'

'There won't be any snow,' said Dad. 'This planet has an artificial atmosphere – I think it'll be like a giant factory.'

'I think it'll be like *Star Trek*,' said Jake hopefully.

'I think it'll just be magic,' said Sadie.

The Trubshaws stepped out of their space cabin into bright daylight and what looked at first like a busy airport. They were on the edge of a huge green airfield, dotted with weird, boxy, wingless planes.

'Those aren't planes,' said Dad. 'They'Re sLeighs!'

A bell clanged loudly, making them all jump.

'Don't be alarmed,' said Captain Crisp. 'It's just the signal to scramble.'

The sleigh that was closest to them was suddenly surrounded by elves in bright green overalls.

'That's the ground crew,' said the captain, smiling proudly. 'Now watch out for the reindeer squadron – here they come!'

He pointed, with his long, spindly finger, at a large hangar a few metres away.

The big doors suddenly burst open and eight tall reindeer galloped out in tight formation, so fast that the humans just caught a glimpse when they thundered past. In a few seconds, as quickly as a speeded-up film, the elves fastened the reindeer into their harnesses, and the sleigh took off into the artificial sky with a great **WHOOSH** and a shower of sparks.

'Why were they all wearing those knitted rasta hats?' asked Mum. 'And – did I really see dreadlocks?'

'All the squadrons like to add a few personal touches,' said Captain Crisp. 'That one is quite famous – they're known as the Three Rs, which stands for the Reggae-Reggae Reindeer.'

'The Three Rs are pretty cool,' said Percy, 'but not as cool as the Jambusters.'

'I thought you said someone would be here to meet us,' said Dad.

'Yes,' said the captain. 'Mr Tolly Blobb, from head office, is waiting for you in the arrivals lounge – sorry the door is so small, but humans are taller than elves and reindeer.'

Sadie, who was the same height as a grown-up elf, skipped easily through the door, and Jake only needed to bend his head. Mum and Dad had to crouch right down.

'Everything's *my size!*' cried Sadie gleefully. 'You two are giants!'

The airport lounge was crowded with elves and reindeer, and the grown-up Trubshaws loomed over them like great trees.

They heard Percy's mum before they saw her.

'PERCIVAL CLIFFORD PRANCER, YOU ARE NEVER GOING OUT OF MY SIGHT AGAIN

AND DON'T TRY TO HIDE BEHIND THOSE POOR HUMANS!'

Mrs Prancer was a stout reindeer, yet she also looked like a cross, worried, busy mum. She had a clump of curly fur on the top of her head, and she wore glasses on a chain round her neck. 'I can't turn my back on you for a moment! Breaking into a sleigh – how could you be so *silly*?'

'Hi Mum,' said Percy sheepishly. 'Sorry.'

A very small reindeer peeped out between Mrs Prancer's legs. 'Ummmm, you've been *naughty*!'

'That's my sister Belinda,' said Percy crossly. 'She's seven, but she's very young for her age.'

'**Pooh!**' shouted Belinda. She stuck out her big, pink reindeer tongue.

'Stop it, both of you,' said Mrs Prancer. She looked up at Mum. 'Mrs Trubshaw, I'm so sorry you had to get mixed up in all this!'

'I'm sure it wasn't all Percy's fault,' said Mum. She sat down on one of the small seats so that she could

talk to Mrs Prancer more easily. 'He's a dear little reindeer with lovely manners.'

Sadie knelt on the floor beside Belinda. 'Hi, I'm Sadie and I'm seven, too.'

'Hi,' said Belinda. 'What happened to your front teeth?'

'They fell out,' said Sadie, grinning to show off her gap. 'That probably doesn't happen to reindeer.'

'Mr and Mrs Trubshaw, welcome to Yule-1.' An elf in a smart suit and tie came up to them and bowed. 'My name is Tolly Blobb and I have orders to take you straight to Head Office.'

'We have to get home,' said Dad. 'I'd like to speak to whoever is in charge here.'

'Yes, of course,' said the elf. 'You'll be meeting FC himself.'

'Who's FC?'

Jake and Sadie cried out together,

'FATHER CHRISTMAS!'

'I told you he was real,' said Sadie.

THREE
Head Office

The four humans and three reindeer drove to Head
Office in a coach with an open top, driven by a reindeer
in a blue suit, because nothing else was big enough for
humans.

'This is so embarrassing,' said Mum. 'I'm enormous
and I'm in my dressing gown – and everyone's staring
at us.'

'You're the talk of the whole planet,' said Mrs Prancer. 'We've never had humans here before and nobody knows how it happened.' She glanced at Dad and whispered, 'Is your husband all right?'

'He's fine,' said Mum. 'He just needs a little time to adjust.'

'Fascinating!' muttered Dad, gazing around at the brightly coloured shops and houses, and the busy crowds of elves and reindeer. Every two minutes a sleigh took off and whooshed over their heads.

'I wish you could meet my husband, Ron,' said Mrs Prancer. 'But he's Chief of Sewage in Sector Five and he couldn't get away.'

'That sounds important,' said Mum.

They were in a bright, warm, indoors city now, with wide streets and grand buildings. Mrs Prancer pointed out a few landmarks as they passed – a giant red-and-white striped helter-skelter, a famous park, a theatre.

'And this is Blitzen Brothers, the reindeer department store. It's where I buy the children's school saddlebags and harnesses. The elves go to Nobbly's across the road.'

'It looks like John Lewis,' said Sadie. 'Except that the models in the window are all reindeer.'

'Blitzen?' Mum murmured. 'Oh, of course, it's just like that poem – "T'was the Night Before Christmas".'

'That's right,' said Mrs Prancer. 'All us reindeer are descended from one of the reindeer in that famous poem – we're all called either Dasher, Dancer, Prancer, Vixen, Comet, Cupid, Donner or Blitzen.'

'But where are all the trillions of presents?' asked Mum. 'I thought there'd be heaps of them!'

'All the presents are processed in the big warehouse that covers most of this planet,' said Mrs Prancer. 'You humans wrap them up, and they come to Yule-1 for their special magic delivery on Christmas Eve.'

The coach stopped outside a big, official-looking building that towered over all the others, with huge doors and gleaming windows.

'Head Office,' said Tolly Blobb the elf. 'Follow me, please.'

'**Oh, help!**' squeaked Percy.

They were all quiet now. Head Office was very grand inside, with thick carpets of dark green and wallpaper

patterned with holly, and there were portraits on the walls of important-looking elves and reindeer. Tolly Blobb led them down a long corridor and knocked on a door at the very end.

A deep voice said, **'Come in!'**

'You mustn't be nervous,' Tolly Blobb whispered. 'He's really very nice.'

He opened the door and they walked into a big, grand office with a huge, carved desk.

'The humans, sir.'

'Thank you, Blobb.'

Someone stood up behind the desk – someone so famous that the Trubshaws all knew him at once. He was wearing an ordinary grey suit instead of the red outfit he wore in pictures, but there was no mistaking his thick white hair, his big white beard, or his kindly, twinkling eyes.

'Father Christmas!' squeaked Sadie.

'Hello, Sadie.' He gave her a special smile. 'Hello, everyone! Please call me FC. And do sit down. This is a very strange situation – normally I'm the only human on Yule-1. When young Percy's microchip was activated, you were all automatically sucked into my private space shuttle.'

'But you've got a flying sleigh,' said Dad. 'Why does Father Christmas need a space shuttle?'

'I still pop back to earth sometimes,' said FC, 'to visit Selfridges Foodhall, or to have tea with the Queen. And there's nowhere to park a sleigh and eight reindeer.'

'Stop it, Percy,' said Mrs Prancer. 'Stop trying to hide behind me! I'm very sorry, FC, this hoo-ha is all his fault, because he can't think about anything but those blessed Jambusters! I have no idea how he *sneaked* into the airfield in the first place . . .'

'There was a hole in the fence,' said Percy. 'We saw it when we went there on a school trip.'

'He didn't bring us here on purpose,' Jake said boldly. 'It was just a mistake – and anyway, I'm glad he did it because this place is amazing.'

'Thank you, Jake,' said FC. 'I know you're interested in outer space from all the stickers I've delivered over the years. And it's nice of you to stand up for your foolish friend.'

'He's my foolish friend, too,' said Sadie. 'Please don't be mean to him!'

Percy stopped tangling himself in his mother's legs and hung his head. 'Sorry, FC.'

'That's OK, Percy.' The great man was trying not to laugh. 'You and your friends—'

'That Fred Dancer and that Eric Splatt!' Mrs Prancer cut in crossly. 'Those two are just as much to blame!'

'You and your friends were very silly and rather naughty,' FC went on. 'But you didn't cause this accident.'

'We . . . we didn't?'

'No, little reindeer.' FC's face was still kind, but he was very serious. 'These humans are here because someone meddled with my computer system – someone who wants to spoil Christmas across the whole universe.'

'Oh, no!' cried Mrs Prancer suddenly. 'Not him again!'

And Percy and his sister both gasped out together,

'Krampus!'

'Yes,' said FC. 'I'm afraid Krampus is back.' He pressed a few buttons under his desk. The painting behind him (of a very wrinkled old reindeer) slid back to reveal a screen. It flickered and a picture appeared – a horrible picture of a scowling black creature, with a hairy human chest and arms, and the legs and head of an evil goat. He had big curved horns and a disgusting long black tongue. 'This is Krampus.'

All the humans shivered at the nasty look on the creature's face.

'I see that you've never heard of him,' said FC. 'You don't know him in your country, but he's famous in other parts of Europe. I'll try to explain as simply as possible. Once upon a time, hundreds of years ago, I was only allowed to give presents to "good" children, and the so-called "bad" children were punished with a visit from Krampus.'

'But that's not fair,' said Mum. 'There's no such thing as good or bad children. They're all the same.'

'Quite right, Mrs Trubshaw!' said FC. 'Nowadays we treat *all* children as good children. There are no more punishments, and that means Krampus is out of a job. I offered him a chance to retrain, but he's still furious.'

'I thought you locked him up in prison,' said Mrs Prancer.

'He escaped,' said FC. 'Krampus is very strong, and he can fly better than any of my reindeer – naturally I was careful about security. But I made the mistake of letting him have a computer. That's how he first met a certain wicked reindeer.'

'But reindeer can't be wicked,' said Sadie. 'They're much too *sweet*!'

'Not this one.' FC pressed a button and the picture on the screen changed to a police mugshot of a scowling reindeer with numbers across his chest. 'His real name is Clarence Comet, but he calls himself Nerkins, which is reindeer slang for a horrible person.'

It was very strange to see a reindeer with such a nasty-looking face.

'He wasn't always a criminal,' said FC. 'He's a computer genius and he designed the system that runs this planet.'

'But that's impossible!' said Dad. 'Reindeer don't know about computers! And what about their hooves – how do they work the keyboards?'

'The keyboards are specially adapted, Mr Trubshaw,' said FC. 'And the reindeer put hoof points over their front hooves. Nerkins used his computer knowledge to steal the wages of all the workers at my warehouse. Naturally I paid them out of my own pocket, but I was very angry – and it wasn't just about the money. Until Krampus made friends with that ghastly reindeer, there was no crime on my planet! It was Nerkins' fiddling that weakened the transporter beam and brought you humans here. Unfortunately, nobody else knows enough about computers to stop him.'

'May I take a look?' Dad could never keep away from a computer. For the first time since their arrival, he was cheerful. FC's computer had a huge, boxy screen and a keyboard like an antique typewriter. Dad pulled up a chair and bashed at the keys. 'Good grief – this thing is *ancient*! It should be in the Science Museum!'

'Excuse me,' said Mum. 'When can we go home?'

'Ah,' said FC. 'Of course I *can* send you back to earth.'

'Well, this has been very interesting,' said Mum, 'but we'd like to get back to our holiday now.'

Father Christmas coughed and looked embarrassed. 'I'm very sorry, but there's a small problem. Our planets exist in different time zones, so that I can deliver presents all year round. And that means it'll be some time before you can go home.'

'Some time?' cried Mum. 'What does that mean? How much time?'

'Three months,' said FC. 'I'm really very sorry.'

'**But . . . three months?**' Mum had turned pale with the shock of it. 'What about our jobs and the children's school? **We can't spend three months in outer space!**'

'It's not quite as bad as it sounds, Mrs Trubshaw,' FC said quickly. 'You'll get back to your planet at the exact same time you left it – the first day of your holiday. So you won't miss a single second.'

'I don't mind,' said Jake. 'In fact, I think it's great. I've always wanted to go into space. And I won't have to say goodbye to Percy.'

He looked at Sadie, waiting for her to start crying as usual – but to the surprise of everyone in her family, she was smiling.

'I don't mind either,' said Sadie. 'I think it'll be fun.'

'But . . . what about your friends?' asked Mum. 'Won't you miss Libby?'

'No,' said Sadie. 'She doesn't share things and she's *mean*. Belinda's much nicer – I've never had a friend who's a talking reindeer.'

'I've never had a friend who's a human,' said Belinda

happily. 'And while you're here you can share all my toys.'

The two seven-year-olds giggled and did the secret hand-and-hoofshake they had just invented.

'Oh, well,' Mum said, looking relieved. 'Maybe it won't be so bad if you two don't mind. But we will need somewhere to live for the next three months. Do you have any houses big enough for humans?'

'You can come and live with us,' said Percy hopefully, 'can't they, Mum?'

'Sorry, dear,' said Mrs Prancer. 'We live in a stable. It's not suitable for a human family.'

'There's a lovely big field next to your stable, Mrs Prancer,' said Father Christmas thoughtfully. 'I can build something on that.'

'**Hooray!**' Percy was so happy that he stood up on his hind legs and did a dance. 'We'll be neighbours!'

'That does sound very nice,' said Mum, smiling at Mrs Prancer. 'Though I don't know what we'll do with ourselves for all that time.'

'This computer system needs a total rethink,' said Dad, gazing at the screen. 'I'm not surprised Nerkins can break into it and mess up your deliveries – a two-year-old could do it!'

'We need to talk, Mr Trubshaw.' Father Christmas was now very thoughtful indeed. 'The children can wait in the playroom.'

press any
key to
enter system

FOUR
The Reindeer Canteen

The playroom was a few doors down from FC's office, and it was fabulous, a riot of dazzling colours, filled with every sort of toy and game. There were shelves of cuddly animals, tricycles, bicycles, spacehoppers and pedal cars. Jake and Percy grabbed a couple of scooters (Jake's was designed for a large elf and only just big enough) and rushed to try out the indoor cycling path.

Percy's scooter was specially designed for reindeer, with a low handle for his front hooves. Sadie and Belinda bounced on spacehoppers (Belinda's reindeer spacehopper was a very odd shape).

When they were all out of breath, they tried a machine that gave out free milkshakes. Jake and Sadie pressed the 'E' button and got cups of chocolate elf milkshake that tasted delicious. Percy and Belinda pressed the hoof-shaped 'R' button and got cups of bright-green-grass reindeer milkshakes. Jake tried some and it tasted like lawn mowings mixed with sugar and dirty snow.

'Look at the computer games!' neighed Percy happily. 'They've got *Delivery Wars 2* and it's not even in the shops yet!'

He pointed one hoof at the big screens around the walls. Jake was mad about computer games and he was fascinated when Percy showed him the different sets of controls for reindeer and elves.

'This is the game I play with my two best friends, Eric and Fred,' he explained. 'You choose your squadron and then you shoot presents at the targets but I choose the Jambusters so you have to pick another one.'

'OK,' said Jake. 'I'll go for the Three Rs, just because I've heard of them.'

'And we can play at level one till you get the hang of it.'

'Make it as hard as you like,' said Jake, grabbing the elf controls, 'because you are about to be *destroyed*!'

Delivery Wars 2 was a lot of fun – when you hit your target the present exploded with a loud ping, and Jake got so involved that he forgot Percy was a reindeer and not one of his friends from school.

At the other end of the playroom was a big ball pit. Sadie and Belinda jumped into the great heap of plastic balls with shrieks of delight. When they were tired

of thrashing about and pretending to swim, they sat in the ball pit with just their heads sticking out and talked about their favourite toys.

'I got a pink bicycle for my last birthday,' said Sadie. 'What about you?'

'I got a set of Janiac dolls,' said Belinda. 'The Janiacs are my best reindeer squadron because they're all *girls* and really beautiful.'

'Why are they called the Janiacs?'

'Because they like books by Jane Austen,' said Belinda. 'And they wear lovely little velvet bonnets.'

'They sound nice,' said Sadie. 'I think they'll be my favourites, too.'

The door of the playroom opened and in came two big food trolleys, pushed by an elf and a reindeer in

white chef's hats. The humans were given bowls of elf porridge, hot and sweet and a lot nicer than it sounded. The two reindeer ate stiff cakes of hay with a warm brown gravy – Jake tried a bit of Percy's, and they all laughed when he had to spit it out.

After lunch Tolly Blobb the elf came to take them back into FC's office.

'Sit down, children,' said Father Christmas. 'It's all sorted out.'

'Where are Mum and Dad?' Jake asked, looking around anxiously. 'What's happened to them?'

'They're fine and you'll see them very soon,' said FC. 'Your mother has gone shopping for emergency supplies, and your father is setting up his new office – he has very kindly agreed to redesign my computer system. He's just what I need to beat Krampus and his wicked sidekick!'

'FC says your temporary house will be ready by teatime,' said Mrs Prancer. 'I'm sure you'll like it. We live in a lovely area called Poffle Glen, well away from the flight paths and very popular with families. Before we go there, however, I'm taking you children with me to work. I'm the catering manager in the reindeer canteen, and Wing Commander Dasher wants to meet the humans.'

* * *

Percy was so excited that he was pale underneath his fur. 'Dasher's the coolest reindeer in history! I'm glad I'm wearing my Junior Jambusters badge today.' He showed Jake the gold badge pinned to his red collar.

'That's their fan club.'

'He's very busy and important,' said Mrs Prancer. 'Make sure you say sorry.'

'Yes, Mum.'

'He sounds a bit like James Bond,' said Jake. 'Except that James Bond's not real – or a reindeer.'

They travelled back to the airfield in a lorry filled with boxes of reindeer food.

'Turbo-cakes,' Jake read. 'What's that?'

'Special high-energy haycakes,' said Percy. 'I don't know what's in them, but the squadrons can't fly in space without them. The Turbo-cakes stop them running out of breath or suddenly disintegrating. They're very expensive and difficult to make, so they're reserved for reindeer who are on active flying duty.'

'Pulling a sleigh full of presents must be difficult,' said Jake. 'How does it feel when you're up there?'

'Windy,' said Percy. 'And scary. I didn't have any Turbo-cake – luckily I was inside the sleigh and there was enough air to keep me going until I fell out.'

'Oh, don't remind me!' cried Mrs Prancer. 'When I think of the danger, it makes my blood run cold! Now Jake's here you'll have a *sensible* friend for a change!'

'But my friends *are* sensible!'

'PERCIVAL, ARE YOU ARGUING WITH ME?'

The little reindeer was sulky. 'No, Mum.'

'I expect *best behaviour*!' said Mrs Prancer. 'That means you, too, Belinda – everyone in my canteen is doing vital Christmas work.'

The reindeer canteen was a large square white building on the edge of the airfield. Jake had expected it to look like stables, but inside it was clean and modern – like any office building, except that the person at the

reception desk was a reindeer wearing pink lipstick
and big hoop earrings.

Every few minutes another sleigh took off from the
giant airfield outside the big windows, and there were
loud messages over the PA:

*'Squadron Leader Norah Cupid to the Briefing
Room . . . Harness Repair Team, please report to the
main dock immediately . . . Pilot Officer Mike Donner,
your cloud-busting kit is ready in Shed Three . . .'*

'This place is mind-blowing!' Jake bent down to whisper in Percy's ear. 'Do you come here a lot?'

'No, this is my first time, too,' Percy whispered back, his black eyes shining with excitement. 'The canteen is *top secret*, and it's even more brilliant than I imagined!'

'Here are your passes, children.' Mrs Prancer gave them all plastic cards, which they hung around their necks. 'Come along, the Jambusters are waiting in the dining room.'

'Oh, wow!' neighed Percy.

Jake was catching his excitement. This building was crowded with busy reindeer – everywhere he looked he saw antlers and dappled brown backs. The strangest thing was that he was beginning to tell them apart, as if they were humans. He wished he had more time to see into the rooms they hurried past – a gym where reindeer trotted on treadmills, a hair salon, even a cocktail bar with a reindeer in a bow tie playing the piano.

The dining room was enormous. There were long tables beside the windows, all crowded with reindeer squadrons. These were the most important reindeer in the Delivery Service and every squadron had its own costume, which was usually a hat.

'**Oooh!**' sighed Belinda, pointing her hoof at a table of lady reindeer who wore hats covered with white flowers. 'The Diving Daisies! My next favourite squad after the Janiacs!'

One of the Diving Daisies called out, 'Hi, humans!'

Suddenly everyone was looking at Jake and Sadie. The reindeer smiled and waved at them as they walked past, but it was embarrassing and Jake felt his cheeks turning red. He wished he wasn't in his pyjamas.

'Something smells funny,' said Sadie.

Jake smelt it too. 'It's a bit like chocolate and a bit like a farm.'

'That's the Turbo-cakes, dear,' said Mrs Prancer.

The Turbo-cakes were big and round, the size of a human dinner plate, and made of some dark, chewy stuff. Jake and Sadie thought they looked disgusting, but the reindeer seemed to love them.

An elf waitress wheeled a big cart of the smelly cakes along the row of tables, and a grinning reindeer in an ordinary suit and tie shouted,

'Two Turbo-cakes, please!'

The elf frowned at him. 'Are you flying tonight, sir?'

'No!' The grinning reindeer burst out laughing. 'Come on, you know me – I'm in charge of the laundry!'

'Your hay is in the central manger, sir.' The elf pushed her cart off to the next table, and the reindeer's friends roared with laughter and said, 'Nice try, mate!'

'Well, if it isn't the stowaway!' said someone.

Percy's lips moved, but not a sound came out. They had reached the Jambuster's table, and he was face to face with his heroes. The Jambusters wore large moustaches, like RAF pilots that Jake had seen in films about the Second World War.

'Hi, I'm Dasher.' Wing Commander Dasher's moustache was the biggest – somehow, even though he was a reindeer, Jake could see that he was very handsome. 'It's great to meet humans who are awake. Normally we only see you when you're fast asleep!'

'We don't see you at all,' said Jake.

'That's because we come and go so fast,' said Dasher with a friendly smile. 'We can deliver the Christmas

presents of a whole street in less time than it takes you to blink.'

'AWESOME!' Jake couldn't imagine anything more thrilling than a ride through space on a superfast flying sleigh. 'How long does it take to do a whole city?'

'Go on, Percy!' hissed Mrs Prancer. 'Say you're sorry!'

'That's OK,' said the debonair wing commander. 'You were very silly to go mucking about with my sleigh, but I'm sure you won't do it again.' He broke off and gave a special smile to Sadie and Belinda, who were both staring at him in dazzled silence. 'Would you girls like to meet my friends, the Janiacs?'

They nodded eagerly.

'They're just about to land,' said Dasher, 'and they'll be happy to give autographs.'

'Oh, that would be nice!' said Mrs Prancer.

'The boys can stay here – I'd like to ask Percy a couple of questions.'

Mrs Prancer hurried off with the two excited seven-year-olds, and Percy sat down at the long table with the Jambusters (the reindeer chairs were a weird shape, and Jake decided to stand).

'Don't worry, Percy!' one of the Jambusters said. 'He's not going to tell you off – are you, skipper?'

'No,' said Dasher. 'Though I probably should. Flying sleighs can be pretty dangerous.'

'We didn't mean to fly.' Percy found his voice at last. 'We only wanted to look inside the sleigh and the gift chute seemed like a good way in.'

'What happened to your friends – why were you alone when we took off?'

'My elf-friend Eric tried to stop me climbing inside,' said Percy. 'And my reindeer-friend Fred tripped and fell over before he could follow me. My mum always says he has four left hooves.'

There were neighing chuckles around the table.

'I wanted to get out,' said Percy, 'but the chute was too small and I got stuck.'

'This might be important,' said Dasher. 'What do you remember about falling off?'

'My bottom was sticking out and it got very cold.' Percy was frowning with concentration. 'Then the sleigh shook very hard – and the next thing I knew, I was in the Trubshaws' chimney.'

'Anything else?'

'I sort of heard something,' said Percy. 'Just before I fell off, there was a strange noise — **HEH -HEH-HEH** — like a mean person laughing.'

A murmur of alarm ran though the other Jambusters.

'I knew it,' one of them said. 'I knew that turbulence we hit wasn't normal, skipper – **that was Krampus!'**

'Yes, it sounds like Krampus,' said Dasher. 'Thanks, Percy – I'll warn all the squadrons to take extra care.'

'Could a human join the Delivery Service?' asked Jake.

'No – sorry,' said Dasher. 'It takes a lot of flying power to pull a sleigh. And humans can't fly.'

'But how do you know – has a human ever tried?'

Before Dasher could answer any more questions,

the waitress came to the table with her cart.

'Are you flying tonight, sir?'

'That's the general idea,' said Dasher. 'Three cakes, please.'

An elf with a large camera arrived and spent a long time taking photos of the Jambusters and Jake, and then Mrs Prancer came back with Sadie and Belinda, who were both beaming with happiness.

'We met the Janiacs and got all their hoofprints!' said Belinda.

'And they gave us these gorgeous badges,' said Sadie, proudly showing Jake a purple-and-gold badge pinned to her pyjamas. 'They're *wonderful*!'

A message boomed over the PA.

'Jambuster Squadron, your sleigh is ready for take-off . . . Jambusters to Shed One.'

'We must go,' said Dasher. 'Come along, chaps – those presents won't deliver themselves!'

It was time to shake the hooves of the heroes and leave the canteen.

The idea of flying had got into Jake's brain and stuck there. 'So how do you do it?' he asked Percy when they were back in the lorry. 'Is it something you're just born with?'

'No,' said Percy. 'We learn how to do it at school.'

'I wish we did stuff like that at my school! How far can you fly?'

'I can't fly at all yet,' said Percy. 'I've only just started. Maybe you could learn with me.'

'Don't get carried away, dear,' said Mrs Prancer. 'Not all us reindeer are natural flyers. I was terrible when I was at school, always bumping into things. And Percy's dad could hardly get off the ground. A human could never do it.'

This was disappointing, but Jake refused to give up. If a human could get to planet Yule-1, who knew what else was possible?

FIVE
A Flying Lesson

It had been a very long, strange day. Jake and Sadie were tired and Sadie was nearly asleep when the lorry dropped them in the pleasant suburb known as Poffle Glen. It was a pretty place, filled with trees and flowers and funny little houses like painted biscuit tins. They had stopped beside a big park with a cafe, a playground and a paddling pool, crowded with elves and reindeer.

'This is Poffle Park,' said Percy's mum. 'Our stable

is just over there in Stomper Street— Oh my blessed antlers, what's that?'

A huge red-and-white-striped tent loomed above the rooftops.

'There's a circus in our garden,' said Percy.

'Wait a bit, that must be your new home!' cried Mrs Prancer. 'The circus tent was probably the only one FC could find that was big enough for humans.'

The striped tent was only a short walk away, in the field next door to the Prancers' stable. It didn't look very welcoming from the outside – but then Mum and Dad came out to meet them, which made it feel much more homelike.

'This is a very posh tent,' Mum told them happily. 'I hate camping, but this is more like *glamping!* We've got nice soft beds and sofas, a huge television and a superb kitchen! And FC sent a beautiful bunch of flowers.'

'There's even a room for my computer,' said Dad.

The human children were so pleased with their luxurious new home that they forgot how tired they were.

'I don't mind living here for three months,' said Jake. 'This is the best holiday *ever!*'

* * *

The strangest thing about waking up the next morning was how much it felt like being at home on an ordinary day. Dad was eating a large breakfast of sausages and fried eggs, which was his favourite meal. 'FC sent us some human food from his own private supply,' he told them, 'including cornflakes and marmalade.' Instead of his grey T-shirt and baggy old jeans, Dad was wearing a bright green top with a big red collar. 'And he had this extra-large elf suit specially made for me. It's very comfortable – though I'm not sure about the pointed hat.'

He put on a pointed green elf hat, which looked so funny with his glasses that Jake and Sadie burst out laughing.

Mum looked worried. 'I'm sorry, but FC has given me a part-time job in the Reindeer Library, and I can't leave you two here on your own. I'm afraid you'll have to go to school with Percy and Belinda.'

'But it's the holidays!' Jake was outraged. 'That's the unfairest thing I ever heard!'

'It's not the holidays here,' said Mum.

'I don't mind going to school if I can play with Belinda,' said Sadie. 'But don't expect me to learn anything.'

There was another argument when Mum showed them the emergency clothes she had bought at Nobbly's the day before and Jake refused to wear his elf suit.

'I'd rather go to school in my pyjamas, thanks.'

'It's what everyone else will be wearing,' said Mum. 'Don't you want to blend in?'

Jake did want to blend in, and he was tired of walking about in pyjamas and slippers. He put on the bright green top, red trousers and green boots, and had to admit that they felt very soft and comfortable, even if they looked ridiculous.

Sadie's elf suit was pink and purple, and she loved it so much that Mum had to pull her away from the mirror to eat her toast and cornflakes.

After breakfast, Percy and Belinda and a crowd of small reindeer and elves came to take their human friends to school.

'Those are just some girls from my class,' Belinda told Sadie. 'I said they could come and look at you. I hope you don't mind.'

'Hi, girls!' said Sadie, smiling down at them all like a film star.

A ripple of whispers ran through the crowd.

'She's so tall!'

'Look at her beautiful long hair!'

'What happened to her front teeth?'

Percy proudly introduced his two best friends to Jake. 'This is Fred Dancer, and this is Eric Splatt.'

Fred was a little round barrel of a reindeer with very

short legs and a big, rather daft smile. 'Hi, Jake.'

Eric the elf was as small as a human toddler, but his green eyes were bright and sharp, and Jake suspected he was quite a lot cleverer than the two reindeer. 'Nice to meet you, Jake. Sorry about the mix-up with the sleigh.'

'That's OK,' said Jake. 'This planet is great.'

They turned into a street that was crowded with elves and reindeer, all talking or neighing at the tops of their voices as they streamed into school.

Poffle Glen Primary School had smaller doors and windows than a school for humans. Otherwise it was a lot like a human primary school – a bright, modern building with a large playground and walls covered with pictures.

The headmistress, an elf named Ms Doobly, welcomed Jake and Sadie with a kind smile. 'It's a pleasure to have you here, and please feel free to join in any of the lessons. They'll all stop staring at you in a minute or two, but they've never seen humans before.'

Jake was nearly knocked over by a crowd of reindeer and elves from Percy's class.

'Stand back!' cried Percy, butting them away with his antlers. 'Give him some room!'

In the classroom, Jake had to perch on a tiny, elf-sized chair. It was embarrassing to be so big, but just as the headmistress had said, everyone quickly got used to him and stopped staring. The teacher was a cross old elf named Mr Clobbins, and he was surprisingly like a cross human teacher.

The lessons, however, were nothing like human lessons. First there was a very easy (to Jake) maths lesson. After this it was history and Jake was interested to hear about the real Rudolf, who did not have a red nose, but had invented a new kind of nose light.

Then it was lunch in a big room with two serving hatches. Percy and Fred joined the reindeer line and got bags of hay. The two humans queued up with the elves for potato pie and cherry cake – which tasted good, if a bit too sweet.

After lunch, the elves and the reindeer had different classes.

'That's because we do different jobs when we grow up,' explained Eric. 'Us elves have lessons in

sleigh maintenance.'

'And we've got basic flying,' said Percy. 'You can watch if you like. Last week I stayed off the ground for nearly four seconds.'

'I didn't get off the ground at all,' said Fred gloomily. 'Ms Vixen said I was too silly.'

'We don't do flying yet,' Belinda told Sadie. 'We've got painting.'

Sadie liked painting and went off with the other seven-year-olds. Jake decided to watch the flying class. It happened outside in the playground. The teacher was a glamorous, sporty, lady reindeer with a big silver whistle on a chain around her neck. She stood up on

her back legs to shake Jake's hand with her hoof.

'How nice to meet a human! My name is Mavis Vixen. OK, everybody, let's show Jake what we can do!'

Ms Vixen blew her whistle. The reindeer shuffled into a straight line. 'Warm-up exercises first – trot on the spot!'

She blew her whistle again and the reindeer began their on-the-spot trotting. 'Hooves up, everybody!'

When the class had finished their warm-up, Ms Vixen pulled a long bench into the middle of the playground. 'Now we're ready to get off the ground. Watch me, please. I want you to jump over the bench, hold in mid-air – one, two, three – then land gracefully on all four legs.'

She gave them a demonstration, making it look easy. Jake watched closely, hoping to pick up a few tips, and soon saw that flying wasn't easy at all. Some of the reindeer in the class could only get themselves a few centimetres off the ground. Some of them couldn't hover in mid-air. Percy couldn't stop hovering and Ms Vixen had to pull him down.

'Do concentrate, Percy! Now, Fred . . .'

Fred managed to get himself off the ground and to hover in mid-air, but he spoiled it by suddenly turning upside down, which looked so funny that Ms Vixen had to blow her whistle and shout,

'STOP LAUGHING!'

'She told me not to flip over again,' Fred said when the lesson was finished. 'But I don't know how I did it in the first place!'

'I can't believe I forgot how to get down,' said Percy crossly. 'At this rate, I'll never be good enough to join the Delivery Service.'

'I don't want to join the Delivery Service any more,' said Fred. 'I've decided to work in my dad's factory when I'm grown up. He makes tinned moss. You don't need to fly to make tinned moss.'

'I didn't think it would be so hard,' said Jake. 'Do elves fly, or is it only reindeer?'

It was the end of the school day and Eric had joined them in the crowded playground.

'Elves can't fly,' he told Jake. 'Our cells are too weak. When I'm grown up, I want to work in the gift warehouse.'

The tall figure that was Mum walked into the playground, looking rather odd in a long purple elf dress and chatting happily to Percy's mother.

'Hi, you two.' She hugged Jake and Sadie. 'It's such a nice afternoon – let's go to the park.'

SIX
Homework

Everyone seemed to be headed for Poffle Park. They walked the short distance in a noisy, chattering crowd of reindeer and elves.

'We always go to the park after school,' Percy told Jake. 'And it's great. You can play football, or paddle in the big pool—'

'Or eat ice cream,' said Fred.

'What if it rains?' asked Jake.

This made Percy and his friends chuckle, as if Jake had asked something very silly.

'It only rains on the first Tuesday of the month,' explained Eric. 'Otherwise it's always sunny. FC controls the weather here.'

'I stay with the Prancers till my mum finishes at the factory,' said Fred. 'Look, that's our advertisement.' He pointed a hoof at a large poster beside the park gates – a picture of a smiling reindeer with a tin of something and the words **'DANCER'S BLACK NORWEGIAN MOSS – THE TEATIME TREAT!'**

'Cool,' said Jake politely. 'What does it taste like?'

'Yummy,' said Percy. 'I like it on a slice of toasted hay. You should try some.'

'Don't,' muttered Eric. 'If you're not a reindeer it's horrible.'

'Thanks,' Jake muttered back, doing his best not to laugh so he wouldn't hurt Fred's feelings. 'I'm learning to steer clear of reindeer food.'

The park had miles of soft green grass, several busy cafés, a huge paddling pool and a wooden climbing trail built high up in the trees. Sadie and Belinda ran straight to the paddling pool, the two mums settled on the grass with cups of tea and Jake and his friends raced around the climbing trail until they were breathless. Mum called them down for ice creams and they sat on the grass to eat them.

'I've got dandelion flavour,' said Percy. 'Do you want a lick?'

His ice cream smelt like a vase of flowers gone mouldy and Jake said, 'No thanks, mate.'

Fred was the first to finish. He licked his mouth with his big pink tongue and stood up. 'I'm going to do my flying homework – I'll show that bossy Ms Vixen!'

The fat little reindeer took a deep breath, rose up about half a metre, wobbled in mid-air for a few seconds, and then suddenly dropped down on his bottom. **'OUCH!'**

'You're nearly there,' said Percy, jumping up eagerly. 'You just have to think about it harder.'

'I'm not good at thinking,' said Fred. 'I need another snack.' He opened a bag of what looked like rotten black conkers. 'Anyone want a chomp-nut?'

'**Look at me!**' Percy rose into the air, hovered for three seconds and made a neat landing. 'Now have another go.'

'I'll just get it wrong again,' said Fred with his mouth full of chomp-nuts. 'Like I always do.'

'Maybe you should stop eating,' suggested Eric.

Fred swallowed what was in his mouth and this time got himself further off the ground. 'Now I'm hovering – one, two – **ARRRGH!**' With a neighing shriek of alarm, Fred suddenly shot up high into the air. '**HELP!**'

'Come down!' shouted his friends.

'**I CAN'T!**' Fred was floating higher and higher. '**HELP!**'

Jake leapt to his feet, jumped up as high as he could, and stretched out his long human arm to grab one of Fred's legs. '**OK, I've got you!**'

Percy and Eric gasped, and Jake suddenly realised that he was several metres above the ground.

This was incredible – he was standing on nothing.

'YOU'RE FLYING!' cried Percy.

Jake fell back to earth with a thump and Fred landed on top of him. It took the human and the reindeer a few seconds to untangle themselves.

'Thanks, Jake,' said Fred. 'I didn't know humans could fly!'

'Nor did I – I mean, we can't,' Jake said shakily. 'I don't know how I did it . . .'

'You only had one lesson,' said Percy. 'You must have a natural talent.'

Jake tried again, but it was much harder when he was thinking about it, and at first he could only get himself a few centimetres above the grass.

'You're probably thinking too hard,' said Eric. 'Last time you did it, you weren't thinking about flying – you were thinking about catching Fred. Maybe you should try catching something else. Does anyone have a ball?'

Fred had a grubby tennis ball at the bottom of his school saddlebag. He threw it high into the air, Jake jumped to grab it, and once again he shot up several metres.

'Look at me!' he gasped. '**I can fly!**' For a few amazing seconds he stayed up in the air, looking down at the astonished faces of his friends, before he wobbled back to the ground. 'Eric, you're a genius!'

'That's elves for you,' said Fred, his mouth full of chomp-nuts. 'They're really clever.'

'Throw it again,' said Jake. 'Throw it higher!'

Before he could try any more flying, however, the blue sky suddenly turned dark grey and big drops of rain began to fall. There were shouts and neighs of alarm across the park as the crowds of elves and reindeer scrambled for shelter.

'What's going on?' cried Eric. 'It's not Tuesday!'

A loud voice rang out, singing very nastily:

'JINGLE BELLS, JINGLE BELLS –
SMELLY POO AND BUM!
YOU CAN WAIT FOR CHRISTMAS
BUT IT'S NEVER GOING TO COME!'

Now there were screams of **'Krampus!'** and panic broke out, with everybody running in different directions and falling over each other. Sadie and Belinda scrambled out of the paddling pool and ran to their mothers.

And then the rain stopped as suddenly as it had started, and the sun came out again.

Everyone in the park was dripping wet. It had rained so hard that Fred's bag of chomp-nuts had filled with water (he tried one and muttered, 'Chewy!').

'I'm soaked!' gasped Jake. 'I thought you said FC controlled the weather!'

There was a buzzing sound, like a hive of huge bees, and something flew across the blue sky – a sleigh, pulled by a squadron of reindeer, that was being chased by a thick black cloud.

'And you said we were off the flight path,' said Jake. 'What's that sleigh doing here?'

He looked at Percy, but the small reindeer and his friends were gaping up at the sky, frozen with horror.

The black cloud got closer and closer to the sleigh, and swallowed it up in a great explosion, right above their heads, that made the whole park shake.

The cloud melted away and the sleigh had disappeared. The blue sky was empty except for seven bright red parachutes, slowly drifting down to the ground.

For a few minutes the crowd in the park stared up at the parachutes in shocked silence before breaking out in a great babble of screams and shouts.

'PERCY, LOOK!' Jake yelled above the noise. 'They're landing on the hill over there!' He pointed to the top of the smooth green hill. 'Come on!'

He ran towards them on his long human legs and was the first to reach the top of the hill, with Percy galloping behind him. While he got his breath back, he watched the reindeer squadron drop down on to the grass with their parachutes billowing around them.

'Oh no!' panted Percy. 'It's the Jambusters!'

'I should have recognised the moustaches,' said Jake. 'But there's only seven of them – shouldn't there be eight?'

And at that moment, one of the Jambusters shouted, 'Where's the skipper?'

SEVEN
Missing

It took a few moments for the terrible news to sink in. Wing Commander Dasher – Percy's greatest hero – was missing.

'He ordered us to bail out,' said one of the Jambusters shakily. 'He must've decided to stay with the sleigh to guard the Christmas presents – he won't let Krampus get them without a fight!'

'Just like the skipper!' said another Jambuster. 'He's so brave!'

'But where is he?' asked Jake. 'Sleighs and reindeer don't just vanish into thin air!'

Percy, trying not to cry, held his head up proudly. 'Wherever he is, that smelly old Krampus will be sorry!'

A recorded message boomed out across Poffle Park

'THE WEATHER ERROR HAS BEEN FIXED . . . PLEASE KEEP CALM . . . FREE ICE CREAMS FOR EVERYONE!'

The panicking crowd immediately calmed down and long queues formed for free ice cream. Before Jake could ask any more questions, a police helicopter landed on the grass beside the Jambusters. Elves and reindeer in blue police uniforms got out and one of them shouted through a loudhailer, **'PLEASE CLEAR THE AREA!'**

Jake and Percy went back down the hill to where their mothers were waiting.

'Oh, Percy, there you are!' cried Mrs Prancer with a worried look on her furry face. 'We should get home – finish your ice creams, girls.'

Sadie and Belinda, both soaking wet from the rain and the paddling pool, licked busily at their ice creams.

'I've finished mine,' said Fred. 'I had a double dandelion.'

'Here's your mother, Fred,' said Mrs Prancer. 'She's early – she must've come straight from work.'

It was easy to spot Mrs Dancer in the chaos. She was the fattest reindeer Jake had ever seen, and she wore a white coat and a white cap that covered her antlers.

'My darling – my baby – are you all right?' She gave a dramatic shriek and flung her front legs around Fred in a big hug. 'Oh, my precious little pooh-cake! I rushed out of the factory as soon as I heard that dreadful explosion! Are you hurt?'

'Hi, Mum,' said Fred. 'I'm fine – just a bit hungry from the shock.'

'Oh, you poor angel. I'll get you a lovely big plate of food!'

'She's rather a fusspot,' Percy told Jake when Fred and his mother had gone. 'Fred gets a bit embarrassed sometimes.'

'I'm not surprised,' said Jake. 'I'd be embarrassed if my mum called me a precious little pooh-cake in front of my friends.'

The crowd of elves and reindeer seemed to have forgotten the attack very quickly – they were now strolling and chatting, distracted by the free ice creams – but Jake could see that this had been a major emergency. The quiet streets of Poffle Glen were suddenly full of blue police uniforms, and there was a group of TV reporters outside the park gates. On the short walk home they saw a house covered with a huge splodge of something black.

'Soot,' said Mrs Prancer grimly. 'Krampus always leaves a trail of black soot.'

'What's Krampus got against Christmas, anyway?'

Jake asked Percy. 'Why does he want to spoil it?'

The small reindeer was very downcast, but trying hard to be brave. 'He just hates humans being happy, and he hates Christmas because it's the happiest time of the whole year.'

'Has anything like this happened before – a squadron being shot down?'

'No,' said Percy. 'Never.'

'I hope it's not our fault.' Jake did not like to think that he and his family might have brought trouble to this lovely planet. 'I'll ask my dad.'

In Stomper Street they found Mr Trubshaw sitting in a deck chair outside the circus tent, and beside him sat a reindeer in heavy glasses who looked like an older, stouter version of Percy.

'Dad!' Percy galloped across the garden to hug him. 'Did you hear the bang?'

'I certainly did,' said Percy's father. 'It nearly blew my antlers off! And the next thing I knew, all the alarms were going off in my sewers.' He held out his hoof to Jake with a kind smile. 'Hi, Jake, nice to meet you.'

'It's not because of us, is it?' Jake asked anxiously.

'I mean, did the attack happen because we're here?'

Both dads shook their heads.

'It wasn't our fault,' said Mr Trubshaw. 'Nerkins was fiddling with that computer long before us humans arrived.'

'If only we knew where Krampus and Nerkins are hiding!' sighed Percy's dad. 'They have some sort of secret lair. That must be where they're keeping Dasher – but try not to worry too much.' He nuzzled Percy's neck with his nose. 'The wing commander will soon sort them out!'

He was so confident that Percy cheered up, and he cheered up even more when his mother came out of the stable wheeling a trolley that was laden with things to eat and drink.

'I brought you out a bucket of beer, seeing as you've had such a hard day.' She lifted a large metal bucket off her trolley and put it down in front of her husband.

'Well, that's very thoughtful, dear!' said Mr Prancer. He turned to Dad. 'I'd happily offer you some, David – but it's reindeer beer and I don't think you'd like it.'

'Thanks, Ron,' said Dad. 'FC very kindly sent me a

few bottles of human beer from his private supply.'

'And he also sent some baked beans and fish fingers,' said Mum. 'I think we should all have a picnic supper here in the garden – it's such a nice evening.'

Everyone liked this idea. Jake and Sadie quickly changed out of their wet elf suits into their pyjamas, and ran outside again to play with their reindeer friends. Sadie and Belinda bounced on Belinda's trampoline, while Jake and Percy practised flying.

In all the excitement, Jake had forgotten to tell his parents about his new-found talent. His mother came out of the tent with a tray of food, and nearly dropped it when Jake floated over her head.

'Nothing to worry about,' said Dad. 'He must have caught something in the atmosphere.'

'What do you mean, *nothing*?' gasped Mum. 'I can't have my children zooming off into the sky! Jake – promise you'll only fly *inside*!'

Jake quickly promised – but it was a promise he didn't mean to keep.

'I'll make sure I only practise when she's not watching,' he whispered to Percy.

'Good luck with that,' Percy whispered back. 'My mum's *always* watching – she's got eyes in the back of her antlers!'

After supper, Sadie made a fuss about going to bed, as she often did at home. 'It's too early, and me and Belinda haven't finished our new game!'

The seven-year-olds were in Belinda's bedroom, playing with the little reindeer's toy tea set.

'We're having a pretend tea party,' said Belinda. 'And we've put out cups and plates and pretend cakes for Krampus and Nerkins.'

'It was my idea to pretend we invited them to tea,' said Sadie. 'Everybody's mean to them because they're naughty, so we're giving them a chance to turn *good*.'

'I wouldn't have tea with those two!' said Percy scornfully.

'Don't take any notice,' said Jake. 'It's just what Sadie always does when she's scared of something. Last time it was a steam engine we saw at a railway museum near our gran's house. She thought it looked nasty – so she made up a game about being kind to it, to turn it into a good engine. But it didn't work.'

'How do you know it didn't work?' snapped Sadie.

'Because next time we went to the museum, that engine looked exactly the same – scary and mean.'

'He might have looked mean,' said Sadie, scowling at Jake, 'but I could tell he wanted to come to pretend tea again. So I'm going to keep inviting him until he gets kind and good!'

'You can't make bad things good just by pretending to invite them to tea,' said Jake. 'And anyway, all the stuff about the engine was only in your imagination. Your silly game won't work with real monsters like Krampus and Nerkins.'

'IT'S NOT A SILLY GAME!'

'Yes it is – they're far too wicked.'

'And a lot more dangerous than some old steam engine!' Percy sighed and touched his Junior Jambusters badge. **'They've kidnapped Dasher!'**

Jake could see how worried his friend was, though he was trying so hard to be brave. 'He'll be OK,' he said stoutly. 'You said it yourself – Dasher's the coolest reindeer in history!'

EIGHT
Sleepover

The disaster was the only thing anyone could talk about next day. Both the newspapers on the planet (*The Reindeer Gazette* and *The Elf Enquirer*) had the same headline: **KRAMPUS KIDNAPS HERO DASHER!** There were big posters of Krampus and Nerkins on the streets of Poffle Glen, above the words, **HAVE YOU SEEN THESE MONSTERS?**

The headmistress made a speech in school assembly. 'FC has ordered us not to panic, but I want you all to be on the lookout for any signs of the criminals, such as *sooty hoofprints*, or sounds of evil chortling.'

That evening, FC appeared on the television news. 'Christmas must not be ruined,' he said sternly. 'As you all know, it's not just about getting presents and eating too much. Christmas is a time of *peace* and *happiness*, the most special time of the whole year, when people have good thoughts and do kind things. I have used my magical powers to replace the presents

that were on the Jambusters' sleigh, and I know
my gallant reindeer squadrons will keep calm and
carry on.'

* * *

The sensation died down after a few days. Though
Dasher was still missing, FC's sleighs carried on
making their Christmas deliveries and life in Poffle
Glen returned to normal. The Trubshaw family got
used to their new routine surprisingly fast. Dad went
off to work each morning, just like he did at home,
and Mum went to her part-time job in the Reindeer
Library. Jake and Sadie went to school with their
friends and played in the park afterwards. There were
no more unscheduled showers of rain.

Jake was fascinated by everything he saw on this
strange planet. There was a school trip to the giant
warehouse where all the world's Christmas presents
were processed, and he was very impressed by the huge
conveyor belts and swarms of busy elves. But nothing
was as fascinating as flying, and whenever his mother

wasn't around, Jake practised until he got good enough to stay up in the air for a whole half hour.

Ms Vixen was impressed. 'I never thought a human could pick it up so quickly – you're ready to try right and left turns now!'

Jake loved flying. He had dreamt of flying since he was little, never thinking he would actually get to do it one day. Every time he flew he felt more confident. He didn't go on about it, however, because he was better at flying than Percy, and his reindeer friend couldn't help being jealous.

'There's no point in humans flying,' Percy said huffily. 'Humans can't be in the Delivery Service. And you won't be able to do it when you go back to your own planet.'

Jake could see how unfair it looked from a reindeer's point of view, and kindly spent a lot of his spare time helping Percy with his flying homework.

'You're definitely getting better, Perce!' he said encouragingly whenever the small reindeer made a mistake.

Percy made a lot of mistakes. He had a habit of going

up too high and not being able to get down again, and during one lesson he was stuck on the school roof for nearly half an hour when his harness got caught in the gutter (he was very embarrassed about this – Ms Vixen had to fly up to set him free, with the whole school watching).

Little by little, however, Percy's flying really was improving. One afternoon, a month after the kidnapping, he made such a good emergency landing in flying class that Ms Vixen said, 'Excellent, Percy!' and gave him a gold star.

'Thanks for everything, Jake,' Percy said while they were walking home from the park at the end of the day. 'This is my first gold star ever – and it was all because of you!'

'I didn't do much,' said Jake, smiling to see his friend so happy.

'I'm sorry I was cross,' said Percy, blushing behind his fur. 'I thought it wasn't fair that you could fly when you're not a reindeer. But your lessons are brilliant.'

'Thanks, Perce,' said Jake. 'You'll soon be better than me – honestly!'

'I don't want to fly just to show off,' Percy said seriously. 'I want to be ready to chase Krampus and Nerkins next time they do something wicked – then I could find Dasher and set him free.'

'That would be great,' agreed Jake. 'My dad says they're getting worse. He had to stay late yesterday because they meddled with the deliveries again – some kids in New York very nearly got boring soap and nail brushes for Christmas instead of toys.'

'My dad was late, too,' said Percy. 'They mucked about with his sewers, and he only just stopped a poo fountain outside Blitzen Brothers.'

'GROSS!' said Jake, laughing. 'You should tell Sadie – a poo fountain would ruin her tea party!'

Sadie and Belinda were still playing their tea-party

game. Every afternoon, as soon as they got home, they hurried off to Belinda's bedroom where the tiny toy cups and saucers were set out on the floor. Both girls got very cross if anyone tried to clear it up, though Mrs Prancer had started to complain about the mess – they had added a lot of pieces of paper with pictures of pretend food for their pretend guests.

On this afternoon, Mr Prancer accidentally stepped on one of the bits of paper. 'Sorry, girls – I thought it was just rubbish.'

'It's not rubbish!' said Belinda. 'It's a delicious pretend trifle. We think Krampus likes trifle. Now you've made a hoofprint and we have to draw another one.'

'You can do it tomorrow,' said her mother. 'It's bedtime.'

Belinda jumped up on her back legs. 'We could have a sleepover – oh, please!'

'**Please–please–please!**' cried Sadie.

'But it's a school night,' said Mum. 'And Belinda lives in a stable, so there's nowhere for you to sleep.'

'I can take my duvet and sleep on the floor – *please!*'

The two mums looked at each other.

'I don't mind,' said Mrs Prancer. 'We're only next door. I'll make sure they don't stay up all night talking.'

'It's not a real school night,' Jake pointed out. 'Technically we're on holiday. And if Sadie's allowed to go off on a sleepover, I think Percy should stay with me.'

'Cool!' Percy's furry face lit up. 'A sleepover in a human's bedroom – wait till I tell Fred and Eric!'

'Oh, well . . .' said Mum. 'If you really wouldn't mind . . .'

It was settled. Sadie grabbed her duvet and pillow and made herself a bed on Belinda's bedroom floor, beside their tea party. Percy's bed on Jake's floor was a bale of straw and a blanket. They had a lot of fun flying up to the ceiling, until Mum firmly told them to come down and go to sleep.

'I can't believe I'm sharing a room with a talking reindeer,' Jake whispered after the light had been turned off. 'Goodnight, Percy!'

Percy yawned. 'Goodnight, Jake!'

* * *

Jake woke up in the middle of a weird dream that he was a car going through a car wash, and found Percy snuffling in his ear and nudging his shoulder with his hard little hoof.

'Jake – wake up!'

'What?' he mumbled. 'What time is it?'

'Shhh!' hissed Percy. 'Keep quiet, or we'll miss him!'

'Who?' Properly awake, Jake sat up in bed. 'What's going on?'

Percy was quivering with excitement. 'Didn't you hear it too? There was a big thump that came from my house – and then I heard *Krampus*!'

'The real Krampus?' Jake swung his legs out of bed. 'Did you see him?'

'I heard him laughing – just like I did when I fell off the sleigh!'

'And you're sure it wasn't a dream?'

'Of course it wasn't!' Percy stamped his back hoof impatiently. 'He's got into our stable, and we've got to get rid of him!'

'All right, keep your antlers on.' Jake pulled on his elf boots. 'Let's take a look.'

The two friends crept out of the circus tent. It was the dead of night, but the lamp post in the street made it light enough to see black splodges on the grass that led into the Prancers' stable.

'Sooty hoofprints!' Percy squeaked. 'I told you!'

'This is weird,' whispered Jake. 'What made them come here?'

In the night-time silence, they heard a strange sound – a low mumble of deep, growly voices inside the stable, as if someone had left a radio on.

As quietly as they could, Jake and Percy crept into

the stable, and the voices were louder. The door to Belinda's bedroom was open, with a strange, pale light spilling out – and when they looked in, they saw something incredible.

The two girls were fast asleep, and there were two dark figures crouched on the floor. One was a reindeer, and the other had horns, a pointed tail and a disgusting long black tongue. Jake and Percy froze with terror, but Krampus and Nerkins had noticed nothing. They were playing with Belinda's toy tea set and seemed to be enjoying themselves.

'Do have a pretend cake, Nerky!' growled Krampus.

'Yum-yum! THanKS, Krampy. Ha Ha Ha!'

Jake was very scared and had no idea what they should do – if they woke the grown-ups or called the police, the two criminals would hear them. For what seemed like ages, they watched Krampus and Nerkins pretending to drink out of the tiny toy cups.

And then Krampus said, 'That was fun! Let's go back to the hideout.'

Krampus and Nerkins stood up, and there was a strong smell of old chimneys as the two most-wanted criminals on planet Yule-1 ran out of the stable in a black cloud of soot.

'Phew!' said Percy, in a shaky whisper. 'They didn't see us.'

'Good!' Jake whispered back. 'Come on!'

'What are you doing?'

'If we follow them we can find their hideout!'

'Are you *mad*?' gasped Percy. 'It's far too dangerous!'

'I'm not frightened,' said Jake.

'Yes you are!'

'OK, yes I am – but there's no time to wake anybody

up, and this might be our only chance!'

Jake followed Krampus and Nerkins outside, with Percy – forcing himself to be brave – close behind him. The criminals were on the lawn now, and they were in no hurry to leave. Percy and Belinda had left a few toys outside, and Krampus and Nerkins were looking at them curiously.

Krampus liked the small trampoline. The scowling creature climbed on top of it and chortled, **'BOUNCY!'**

Nerkins jumped on to Belinda's pink spacehopper. **'EVEN BOUNCIER!'**

They began to bounce, but the toys were too small for them. Krampus fell through the trampoline and got the metal frame stuck round his waist.

'HA HA HA!' giggled Nerkins. 'You're stuck – **OW!'** The spacehopper burst with a loud POP and all the air rushed out of it.

'Big fart noise!' chortled Krampus – and both creatures burst out laughing.

'I think I know why they haven't noticed us,' Jake whispered in Percy's ear. 'They're too busy *playing*!'

NINE
Night Ride

It was very strange to see that Krampus and Nerkins liked playing, but there was no time to wonder about it now.

'Come on, Nerks,' growled Krampus. 'Let's go home.'

'OK,' the wicked reindeer growled back – and the two criminals rose into the air in another cloud of soot.

'This is our chance!' Jake hissed at Percy from their hiding place behind a big dustbin. 'If we follow them, we'll find their secret lair!'

Percy let out a strangled shriek of alarm. 'What are you doing? We can't follow them. You know my flying is *rubbish*. We have to wake up Mum and Dad. I'll never get off the ground—'

'Shut up,' said Jake breathlessly. 'You're already flying.' He had grabbed Percy's collar and dragged the wriggling reindeer up into the air. 'Just keep your eyes fixed on them, and don't let them out of your sight!'

'What?' gasped Percy. 'What do you mean—? Oh, *crumbs* – I'm flying!'

He began to fall but Jake had a tight hold on Percy's collar and gave him a shake. 'Look at the black cloud – that's what I'm doing. Don't you want to find Dasher?'

'Yes, but I didn't think it would be so *scary*!'

'Pull yourself together, Perce!' Jake said firmly. 'We don't have time to be scared.'

Jake was very frightened, but forced himself to fix all his attention on the black cloud in front of them.

Percy wriggled and squeaked a bit more, and then

began to fly properly. 'Thanks, Jake – you can let go of my collar now.'

Jake dared to let go, and the two of them were flying side by side through the chilly night air. It was incredible to see the lights of Poffle Glen falling away behind them – if they hadn't been concentrating so hard, it would have been brilliant.

There were more lights now as the sooty cloud hurtled towards the town.

'Where are they going?' panted Percy. 'The secret hideout can't be here— **LOOK OUT!**'

A sleigh shot past in a shower of sparks, nearly blowing them off course.

'We're on the flight path!' gasped Jake. 'We'd better fly lower down – quick, before the next one!'

The human and the reindeer dropped down until they were only a few metres above the still, silent streets of the town.

The black cloud that was Krampus and Nerkins halted in mid-air so suddenly that Jake and Percy had to duck behind the roof of Blitzen Brothers.

'They haven't seen us,' whispered Percy.

'This must be their secret lair,' Jake whispered back. 'I didn't think it would be in the middle of town!'

Krampus and Nerkins landed at the top of the big helter-skelter that Jake had seen when he first came to Yule-1.

'But it can't be!' said Percy. 'This is where I had my birthday party – maybe they're playing again.'

'Whatever,' said Jake. 'We can't lose sight of them now!'

'WHEEEEE!' yelled Krampus, whizzing down the helter-skelter.

'WHEEEEE!' yelled Nerkins, jumping on behind him.

Jake and Percy flew to the

top of the helter-skelter. Jake grabbed a mat with one hand and Percy's leg with the other – the small reindeer had forgotten how to get down again and Jake had to pull him.

'Thanks!' said Percy.

The two of them hurtled down the giant helter-skelter – if they hadn't been chasing criminals it would have been incredible fun. They reached the soft mattress at the bottom a minute after Krampus and Nerkins. For a moment, Jake was sure they were going to crash right into them, but they pulled up a trapdoor in the floor and vanished through it.

'So they're not hiding inside,' said Percy. 'They're underneath.'

'What's under here, then?' asked Jake.

'I don't know – it's the inside of the planet.'

There was a dim light inside the helter-skelter. Jake got down on his knees and found the handle to the trapdoor. He opened it, and they both stared down into a dark tangle of shadows.

'I'm really scared now,' said Percy in a wobbly voice. 'Maybe we should stop and call the police.'

'We can't give up when we're so close!' Jake was scared too, but also very excited. 'Come on!'

The trapdoor opened on to a long metal staircase. Jake took a few deep breaths to steady his nerves, then began to walk carefully down the stairs.

'Oh, help!' muttered Percy, climbing through the door after him.

Jake knew that the inside of his own planet was filled with red-hot molten rock, but the inside of Yule-1 – as far as he could make out in the pale light – was a complicated mesh of scaffolding and metal stairs covered with dust. At the bottom of the stairs there were more stairs, and then they caught a glimpse of Krampus and Nerkins ahead of them, hurrying though a door.

'They haven't seen us,' Jake whispered in Percy's ear. 'They've left the door open.'

The light was stronger now. Jake crept through the door behind Krampus and Nerkins, and nearly gasped aloud with surprise. They had come to a big underground chamber. In the middle of this was something large and boxy – a sleigh, heaped with parcels and surrounded by crumpled wrapping paper.

'That's the Jambusters' sleigh!' whispered Percy. 'I don't know how they got it down here, but I'd recognise it anywhere!'

'What's that big mess of wires?' Jake pointed to a tangle of wires, plugs, keyboards and cracked screens which was spilling out of one corner of the chamber.

'It looks like a collection of broken computers! Don't tell me that's what Nerkins has been using!'

Krampus and Nerkins – with no idea they were being watched – burst out laughing and jumped on the stolen sleigh. They had pushed back the huge pile of Christmas presents and made themselves beds with heaps of grimy duvets that looked as if they had been rescued from dustbins.

'Give us a parcel,' growled Nerkins. 'Let's see if there's something to eat!'

Frozen with amazement, Jake and Percy watched the criminals as they started to rip the paper off the nearest parcels. They were opening the stolen Christmas presents.

These presents had been chosen with care and wrapped up with love, and it was dreadful to see them being rudely ripped apart and tossed aside.

After a few minutes Nerkins's antlers were festooned with bits of frilly silk underwear and Krampus was soaking his hooves in a large plastic foot spa. They had a pretend fight, squirting each other with bottles of perfume and aftershave. Nerkins found a chocolate orange and threw it into his mouth with the packaging still on. Krampus gobbled up a fruit cake and the tartan tin it came in.

And then – just as Jake was wondering what they should do – Krampus suddenly raised his head and took a deep sniff.

'I smell HUMAN!' he roared.

'YUK!' shouted Nerkins.

It happened so fast that Jake and Percy had no chance to get away. The two monsters pounced on them and dragged them out into the middle of the underground chamber.

'Well, well!' chuckled Krampus. 'What have we here? Is this the best FC can do – a human boy and a very small reindeer? It'll take a lot more than that to stop us!'

'Two more *heroes*!' sneered Nerkins. 'Company for the other one!'

Jake was very frightened now, and he felt Percy trembling beside him. It was horrible to see Krampus's yellow eyes and goatish face close up.

'You . . . You won't get away with this!' he gasped, trying to sound brave. 'Let us go, or you'll be sorry!'

'But we *have* got away with it!' growled Nerkins. 'So pooh to you!'

The wicked reindeer unlocked a metal door in the wall with a large key he wore around his neck, and Krampus threw Jake and Percy into a dark prison cell.

'Come on, Nerks, we don't have time to chain them up now.'

In the darkness they heard a flurry of hooves, and then there was deep silence.

'I think they've gone,' whispered Jake. 'Are you OK, Perce?'

'I . . . I don't know!' Percy said shakily. 'What're we going to do now? Nobody knows where we are!'

This was an awful thing to think about.

'Sorry,' said Jake. 'Maybe we should have told someone.'

Out of the shadows a faint voice said, 'The human and the stowaway?'

Jake's eyes were getting used to the dark, and he could see a shape in one corner of the cell. 'Who's there?'

'DASHER!' cried Percy.

'Yes, it's me,' said the voice. 'I'm very weak – I've had nothing to eat, except all the leftover chocolates they don't like.'

'We wanted to rescue you,' said Percy sadly. 'But now we need rescuing, too!'

'This is a bit of a disaster,' said Jake. 'And it's my fault. Do you know where they've gone?'

'They're planning something pretty big,' said Dasher. 'I don't know what. But there is something you boys can do for me – quick, before they come back. When we were shot down, I managed to hide something under my collar. I can't reach it because they chained my hooves – it's a small parcel wrapped in tinfoil.'

'I'll get it for you!' Jake could now see the outline of the wing commander. He scrambled across the floor and his human hands quickly found the squashy tinfoil parcel.

'It's a Turbo-cake,' said Dasher. 'Just what I need to make me strong again!'

Jake opened the parcel and out wafted the familiar smell.

'Mmmm – delicious!' said Percy.

'**Eeyew!**' said Jake, staring at the disgusting black mess that was stuck to the tinfoil.

'Put it next to my mouth,' said Dasher. He licked up the Turbo-cake in one gulp. 'Now, stand back!'

The captured wing commander suddenly reared up on his hind legs and broke his chains as if they had been made of paper. 'That's better!' His voice was back to its normal strength. 'At last I can fight again – thanks to both of you.'

'What do we do now?' asked Jake.

'We wait,' said Dasher cheerfully. 'Those two criminal geniuses aren't as clever as they think!'

TEN
Grounded

The cell was warm and dark, and Jake and Percy – feeling much safer now they were with Dasher – fell asleep. Jake didn't know how long he had been sleeping when the wing commander woke them up.

'Shhh!' he whispered. 'They're back – keep as still and quiet as you can!'

They all listened fearfully to the sounds on the other side of the door.

'Ha Ha Ha – THiS WiLL FiX THEM!' cried

Krampus. 'How long will it take?'

'It has to boil for ten minutes,' said the voice of Nerkins. 'Let's have some of those *special* chocs while we're waiting.'

'Excellent!' whispered Dasher. 'They're crazy about those liqueur chocolates that have alcohol inside – in a few minutes, they'll be *drunk*!'

There were sounds of tearing paper, followed by sounds of guzzling, and then some snatches of singing.

'Yuk, these pies are mouldy – let's give them to the prisoners!' growled Krampus.

'Keep still,' whispered Dasher.

The door opened suddenly, filling the cell with pale light. Jake and Percy, trembling with fear, kept as still as they could.

'Dinner Time!' Nerkins came to the door and threw in a squashed cardboard box of broken mince pies. **'Yum yum!'**

Behind him, Jake could see the stolen sleigh. The drunken criminals had made a small fire on the stone floor, and hanging above it was a bubbling cauldron of something dark and gloopy.

'I think it's ready,' said Krampus. 'Come and help me put it in the spray-bottle – quick, or we'll miss our chance!'

'You do it,' said Nerkins. 'I've only got hooves.'

He turned away – forgetting to shut the door – and Jake and Percy watched as the two criminals stood over their cauldron.

'This stuff had better work!' said Krampus.

'Of course it'll work,' snapped Nerkins. 'I got the recipe off the Magic Internet.'

'Come on, then – give us a hand with the sack.'

Krampus pushed the rest of the heap of gifts off the sleigh and Nerkins dragged a large sack of coal across the floor with his mouth – Jake had no idea what they were doing, but he heard Dasher catch his breath and mutter, **'Those fiends!'**

After another interval of tuneless singing, Krampus and Nerkins climbed on to the Jambusters' sleigh.

'Get on my back,' whispered Dasher, 'and do exactly as I tell you.'

This was scary, but there was no time to think about it. Jake and Percy scrambled on to Dasher's back, holding tight to his collar.

'NOW FOR THE CAKES!' cried Krampus.

The wicked reindeer had a plastic box of something black and sticky that both criminals lapped up greedily. The underground chamber filled with a familiar stench.

'They've got Turbo-cakes!' gasped Dasher. 'Hold on, boys!'

The stolen sleigh began to move, and Jake remembered what FC had said about Krampus flying better than any reindeer – he could make the sleigh move by itself. As quickly as a gust of wind, Dasher ran out of the cell and leapt on to the back of the sleigh. He landed on the heap of duvets and burrowed underneath them – luckily, the criminals were too drunk to notice.

The sleigh picked up speed and Jake dared to peep out of the duvet heap to see where they were going. For the first few minutes they rattled through the metal stairs and walkways on the inside of Yule-1. Then there was a rush of cold air, and they were flying over the streets of the town.

'We're headed for the airfield,' said Dasher, no longer whispering. 'What do those drunken idiots think they're doing?'

The sleigh dived towards the ground – so suddenly that Jake was sure they were about to crash – and landed with a mighty **THUMP** on a lonely country road.

'It's not here, you **FURRY FOOL!**' growled Krampus.

'Yes it is!' growled Nerkins. 'So *bum* to you!'

They climbed off the sleigh and Jake dared to peep out from under the musty heap of old duvets.

A large lorry was making its way along the road.

Nerkins jumped in front of it and roughly pulled the reindeer driver out of his seat. Krampus wrenched open the back doors and sprayed something at the boxes inside.

'Ha ha ha!' he roared. **'WE DID IT!'**

He tied up the hooves of the driver, and then he and Nerkins did a drunken dance.

'This is a disaster!' hissed Dasher. 'I can't be sure, but I think they've just poisoned a whole load of Turbo-cakes – the cakes for all the deliveries next Christmas!'

'Call the police!' squeaked Percy.

'No time,' said Dasher. 'We've got to stop them – or next Christmas will be *cancelled*!'

'But that's impossible,' whispered Jake. 'Isn't it?'

'I'm afraid not,' said Dasher. 'It takes a long time to make Turbo-cakes, and without them all FC's sleighs will be grounded. That means there won't be any presents, and the earth's calendar will jump forward to an ordinary day in January – a school day!'

It was horrible to think about – a long winter with no Christmas, no holidays, no presents. Jake felt Percy trembling beside him.

'The sack of coal says it all,' whispered Dasher. 'In the old days, Krampus used to punish so-called naughty children by putting lumps of coal in their shoes, instead of giving them presents.'

'Isn't there anything we can do?' asked Jake.

'We might have a chance,' said Dasher. 'Jake, I need your human hands.'

'OK.'

'Crawl to the front of the sleigh and get their box of Turbo-cakes – they haven't sprayed those with their poison.'

There was no time to be frightened. Jake clambered quickly across the pile of presents and grabbed the plastic box of Turbo-cakes – luckily the two criminals were too busy laughing and dancing to notice.

Dasher opened the box and gobbled the last of the cakes.

'Now I'm superstrong and you two can get off this sleigh. Untie the van driver, then go straight to FC to give him a full report.'

'But what about you?' asked Percy.

'My place is here, but it's going to be dangerous.'

'Can't we stay?' asked Jake. 'We might be able to help—'

Before he could finish the sentence, Krampus and Nerkins jumped back on the sleigh, and Krampus yelled, **'DELIVERY TIME!'**

The stolen sleigh took off with a tremendous jolt that threw Percy, Jake and Dasher against the sack of coal.

'I spoke too soon,' gasped Dasher. 'Hold tight – these idiots are terrible drivers!'

Jake clutched the side of the sleigh with one hand and Percy's hoof with the other. They were travelling fast, but with a lot of violent wobbling – Jake looked out from under the duvet heap, trying not to feel sick as they zigzagged over the lights of the town.

'It's too heavy,' growled Krampus. 'We'd better get rid of those presents!'

There was a sudden rush of cold air and Dasher cried out, **'They've opened the gift chute!'**

The three stowaways shot out of the sleigh – it felt like being spat out of a giant's mouth – and plummeted towards the ground.

'**FLY!**' shouted Dasher. 'Fly for all you're worth!'

Jake and Percy were too terrified to do anything but scream, but the wing commander held them with his hooves and slowed them down, just before they hurtled through an open skylight in the roof of a large building and landed in a huge vat of something warm, soft and squelchy.

'You were very lucky,' said Father Christmas. 'You could have been seriously hurt – if you hadn't fallen through the open window at Dancer's factory and landed in a gigantic tub of black moss!'

Jake, Percy and Dasher were in FC's private office at the airfield, and Jake's head was still spinning from the disgusting experience of nearly drowning in the warm black moss. Two reindeer security guards had heaved them all out of the tub, hosed off the moss and raised the alarm. Father Christmas looked strange in striped pyjamas and a dressing gown. It was also strange – and scary – to see the jolly old man so worried.

'This is very bad,' he said. 'I've been doing this job for a very long time – and this could be the first time I've lost a Christmas! By the time I've made more Turbo-cakes it'll be too late to save it.'

'Sorry I couldn't stay with my sleigh,' said Dasher. 'Now there's no way to find out where they're going.'

'Never mind,' said FC. 'You three were extremely brave – Jake and Percy, I've told your parents you're safe and they're coming to collect you.'

'Thanks,' said Jake.

'I hope they're not too cross,' said Percy.

'We haven't lost yet,' said Dasher, 'There must be *something* we can do!'

'The Turbo-cakes for next Christmas have been poisoned and my squadrons are grounded,' sighed FC. 'Where are Krampus and Nerkins going?'

'They don't have enough magic to work alone,' said Dasher. 'So who is the wicked creature that's helping them? You know they can't do a thing without a contact on the ground!'

'A contact?' Jake was bewildered. 'What kind of contact?'

'Someone – or *something* – who practises bad magic,' said FC. 'I've no idea who, but my boffins are working on it now.' He pressed a button under his desk. 'Send in Professor Rudolf!'

A moment later there was a knock on the door and a reindeer came into the office – the oldest, wrinkliest reindeer that Jake had ever seen, with glasses perched on his grey muzzle.

'Rudolf!' he blurted out.

'The Real Rudolf!'

'That famous song has given you humans the wrong idea about me,' said the professor. 'Ever since I came up with that nose light one foggy Christmas Eve. Now you all think I have a red nose that glows in the dark, which is obviously ridiculous. I'm actually the best scientist on this planet.'

'Oh,' said Jake. 'Sorry.'

'Well?' asked FC. 'Have you made any progress?'

'A little,' said Rudolf. 'The earth is very big and Christmas covers it like a huge blanket – but I'm getting some weird signals. It seems that part of the earth has been *unChristmassed*!'

'What does that mean?' asked Jake.

It sounded awful, but for the first time, FC smiled. 'It means we can pinpoint the location of anti-Christmas activity!'

'The dark patches of bad will are in the UK,' said Rudolf. 'In the Norfolk-Suffolk area.'

FC pressed another button, and the screen behind his desk showed a map with a black streak across it. The map changed to a photo of a motorway. It looked like any other motorway, except for a large and ugly concrete water tower.

'**Hey – I know that!**' Jake said. 'We drive past it on the way to my gran's house!'

Everyone was looking at him now.

'Is your gran an evil monster?' asked Percy.

'No!'

'Think carefully, Jake,' said FC. 'Have you ever heard about bad magic in that area? Are there any local witches or demons that people tell stories about?'

'No,' said Jake. 'It's just a quiet place in the country – near the railway museum, where we saw the steam engine that gave Sadie nightmares.'

'A steam engine!' FC cried. 'This could be important – what do you remember about this engine?'

Jake was a little embarrassed – it sounded so babyish. 'Well, we go to that museum whenever we visit Gran. When I was really little I liked books about Thomas the Tank Engine and there's a big statue of Thomas beside the road – but he's not bad. There's a shed full of antique engines, including a big black thing that was built in Germany in the 1930s – my dad said the Nazis designed it to look scary. All the other engines look kind.'

'Well done, Jake!' said FC. 'At last we know where those two are headed – the famous steam museum at Bressingham!'

'You mean . . . Sadie was right? She pretended to invite them to tea, but I thought she was just making up stories!'

'Not at all,' said FC. 'Your little sister has a very

sensitive imagination. She somehow knew that engine was bad. And the engine might have given Krampus and Nerkins a sign that it was bad!'

'But it's not much use knowing where they've gone,' said Dasher, 'when none of your squadrons can fly.'

'If I can get just *one* sleigh into the air, there's a chance of stopping them,' said FC cheerfully. 'How about it, Professor?'

'I think I can give you that one sleigh,' said Rudolf.

'Hooray!' cried Dasher, jumping up on his back legs. 'Let me have it, FC – for me and the Jambusters! I got the last of the unpoisoned cakes.'

'It's not as simple as that,' said Rudolf. 'I tested that poison, and ran it through my DNA database to find reindeer who were immune to it. I only found seven.'

'That's all I need,' said FC. 'Which squadron are they from?'

'It's not just one squadron,' said Rudolf. 'Here, I made a list of everybody not affected.' He handed a piece of paper to Father Christmas, who stared at it in silence for a long time.

'Dasher, you must lead this special squadron,' he said eventually. 'You're there because you didn't eat any poison. And there's another Jambuster who isn't affected by it – Ginger Blitzen.'

'Good old Ginger!' cried Dasher. 'Who else?'

'His sister Lucy,' said FC, 'from the Janiacs. Harriet Donner, from the Diving Daisies, and Algernon Comet from the Three Rs.'

'That's five,' said Dasher. 'What about the other three?'

FC sighed. 'I don't like this at all. The other three aren't in any squadron, and one of them isn't even a reindeer – Jake and Percy.'

It took a moment for this to sink in. Jake and Percy stared at each other.

'Us?' squeaked Percy. 'We can't fly a sleigh!'

'I'm a human,' Jake pointed out, his heart thumping with excitement. 'But I can fly a bit – and I'd love to be part of a real delivery squadron!'

'I know it's a lot to ask,' said FC. 'And I know you'll do your best.'

'They're both pretty good,' said Dasher, smiling at his two rescuers. 'Nothing I can't work with! Who's the last one?'

'This must be a mistake!' FC stared helplessly at the list. 'It says, Fred Dancer!'

ELEVEN
The History Makers

'Fred?' If he hadn't been so shocked, Jake would have burst out laughing. 'Are you sure?'

'That is the name my computer came up with,' said Rudolf. 'Fred Dancer, son of the tinned moss king, nine and a half years old, currently at Poffle Glen Primary School. Do you know him?'

'He's one of my best friends,' said Percy. 'But he's not exactly brilliant at flying – he's even worse than I am! And I don't think I'm nearly good enough to pull a sleigh.'

'You were good enough to rescue me,' said Dasher.

'Yes – but I was very scared all the time.'

'You were scared and yet you did it anyway,' said Father Christmas. 'That's what heroes do!'

'Is it?' Percy didn't look very heroic, but rather small and nervous.

'Just think of this,' said FC, 'you'll be making history!'

'That's a great name for my emergency squadron,' said Dasher. **'The History Makers!'**

* * *

The corridors of the reindeer canteen were lined with cheering reindeer and elves when Dasher took Jake and Percy to the main embarkation shed. This made them both very proud, though they were trembling with nerves. It was a strange and terrible thing to see the airfield dotted with the sleighs that could not be flown.

Just outside the shed, Mrs Dancer was waiting with a bundle of jerseys and scarves that turned out to be Fred.

She gave a tearful shriek when she saw Father Christmas. 'Oh, FC – my poor, delicate baby can't fly through space, not with his weak chest!'

'Mnnn–nffff,' said Fred, through a mouthful of woolly scarves.

Jake's dad and Percy's mum had also come to see them off, and Percy's mum tried to comfort Mrs Dancer.

'Now, Eileen, there's no need to make a fuss! FC will take care of them.' She gave Percy a kiss. 'I'm very proud of you!'

'Thanks, Mum,' said Percy.

Mr Trubshaw hugged Jake.

'And I'm proud, too – who knew you'd spend your summer holiday saving next Christmas? Good luck!'

'His stomach's weak!' cried Fred's mum. 'It's very bad for him to be hungry!'

She was still wailing when they all went into the shed and the doors closed behind them.

'Welcome, Fred!' said Dasher. 'Don't worry about anything – I'll soon turn you into a champion flyer!'

'**Mnnn-nffff.**' Fred unwound his scarves and took off his woolly hat. 'My mum's the worried one. She made me eat three breakfasts! But I'm fine.'

'Good for you, little reindeer!' said Father Christmas. 'Dasher will give you a quick lesson in sleigh management. Luckily, you'll be flying with some of the best reindeer in the service.'

The shed was huge, and empty except for a single sleigh, which was already packed with sacks of Christmas presents. FC left the wing commander in charge and Jake looked around at the other members of this very special squadron.

Ginger Blitzen, from the Jambusters, shook hooves with Percy, Jake and Fred. 'Hi, guys! This is my sister Lucy.'

Lucy Blitzen wore the small velvet bonnet that was the special costume of the Janiacs, and though she was

a reindeer, Jake could see that she was very pretty.

'Hi Jake and Percy! I believe I've met your sisters. Hi, Fred!'

'I'm Harriet Donner,' said the other lady reindeer, who wore the flowered hat of the Diving Daisies. 'Nice to meet you.'

'And I'm Algernon Comet, from the Three Rs.' He wore an extra-tall knitted rasta hat over his dreadlocks, and looked very cool.

'Algernon!' gasped Fred, his eyes shining in his fat, furry face. 'I'm Fred Dancer – and I'm in your fan club!'

'Great!' Algernon shook his hoof. 'When this is all over, you must come to tea with the whole lot of us.'

'Ah, here's the harness team!' said Dasher.

A group of four elves in bright-green overalls had

come into the shed, carrying a tangle of red leather harnesses. A special harness had been designed for Jake – a strange-looking contraption like a scarlet life jacket, which had long straps that fastened to the central harness. There were also straps that fitted round his wrists and ankles.

'But I can't fly like this,' Jake protested. 'I have to move my arms and legs!'

'Don't worry about it, Jake,' said Lucy Blitzen. 'You won't feel the straps when we're airborne. They'll make you prance in time with the rest of the crew.'

'Prance? I don't know how to prance!'

'Honestly, there's nothing to it.' Lucy went to help Dasher and Algernon push the sleigh through the big doors and out on to the airfield.

Before Jake could follow, one of the elves rammed a helmet on his head.

'Sorry,' said the elf. 'We had to put your Rudolf lights on a special helmet because you don't have the right sort of nose.'

'Oh . . .' Jake saw that all the reindeer had bright lights clipped to the ends of their noses. 'Thanks.'

'We'll start with a practice flight,' said Dasher when they were all standing round the sleigh. 'Who's got the Turbo-cakes?'

Ginger held out a smelly plastic bag. 'Here they are, skipper. They might taste a bit odd, but that's the poison – and we're all immune to it.'

'**WOW!**' whispered Percy. 'Real Turbo-cakes!' He quickly ate one. 'That's *delicious*! I feel stronger already!'

'**YUM!**' cried Fred. He gobbled up his Turbo-cake and immediately turned upside down. '**Whoops!**'

'Do I have to?' Jake looked at the sticky black cake, trying not to let the smell make him sick. 'Do they work on humans?'

'Sorry, Jake,' said Dasher. 'You need this to fly in space.'

'OK.' Jake took a deep breath and bravely ate his Turbo-cake. For a few seconds he was sure he was going to throw up, but then the sick feeling went away, a mighty surge of strength ran though his body, and he shot several metres into the air. '**That's amazing!**'

'I'll take the front position with Ginger,' said
Dasher. 'Lucy and Algernon, you'll fly behind us. Fred
and Harriet, you'll fly as five and six. Jake and Percy,
you'll be at the back.'

Thanks to the Turbo-cake, Jake was no longer scared
– just incredibly excited. His dream had come true. He
was part of a real squadron in the Delivery Service.

'Attention, History Makers!' said Dasher's voice
through the earpiece inside Jake's helmet. 'At my
command, we'll go once around the airfield and try a
classic rooftop landing. Squadron, lift off!'

Jake leapt into the air and it felt wonderful. He
was as light as a cloud, yet with a hundred times his

normal strength. And he suddenly understood what
Lucy had said about the prancing – the straps kept his
arms and legs in perfect time with the others. This was
the closest a human could get to being one of the most
important reindeer in the universe.

The new squadron flew round the airfield at
superspeed – their graceful landing only spoiled at the
very last moment by Fred suddenly starting to spin so
fast that he got tangled in his harness.

'What happened there?' Dasher asked, laughing to
see the fat little reindeer being untangled by Harriet.

'Sorry!' gasped Fred. 'It's just that I'm not used to
everything being easy – I was wishing my teacher Ms

Vixen could see me! And next thing I knew—'

'Never mind, we'll do it again,' said Dasher. 'Fred, keep your mind on the job!'

They flew once more around the airfield, and this time everything went perfectly.

'I was worried that the sleigh would be too heavy,' said Percy. 'And once we got going I hardly felt it at all!'

'We haven't tried it in outer space yet.' Jake had wanted to fly through space for as long as he could remember, but now that the dream was about to turn into reality, he was getting nervous – would those Turbo-cakes really be enough to protect him?

'Jolly good, History Makers!' said Dasher's voice over the radio. 'Now stand to attention and look smart, because the *boss* is riding along with us tonight – in person!'

There was an outbreak of cheering. Jake strained round in his harness to see a great crowd of reindeer and elves surging on to the airfield. The cheers got louder, the crowd parted, and a tall figure in red walked towards the sleigh. It was Father Christmas,

magnificent in his most famous costume of scarlet velvet edged with snow-white fur. His hair and beard were as white as the fur and his blue eyes sparkled.

Before Father Christmas climbed on to his sleigh, he patted and stroked his new squadron and shook Jake's hand. 'I'm very grateful for your help, Jake. The criminals think my entire fleet has been grounded. They're about to get a very nasty surprise!'

'I thought you rode on all the sleighs,' said Jake.

'I can see that you're confused,' said FC. 'I'm on every sleigh in *spirit*, and today I'm also in the flesh.'

'Are we getting oxygen cylinders?'

'You won't need oxygen,' said FC. 'For the next few hours, you're not a human, but an *honorary reindeer*!'

'Oh . . . good.' Jake could only hope the great man knew what he was doing.

Father Christmas took his place at the front of the sleigh, and cried out in a voice that boomed across the airfield:

'Now **DASHER,**
now **GINGER!**
Now **HARRIET** and **DANCER!**

On, **LUCY!**
On, **COMET!**
On **TRUBSHAW** and **PRANCER!**

To the top of the porch! To the top of the wall! Now dashaway! Dashaway! Dashaway all!'

There was a great gust of wind, and suddenly the
sleigh was flying.

TWELVE
Saving Next Christmas

The feeling was even better than Jake had imagined. He was part of a real delivery squadron, hurtling towards the artificial sky of Yule-1 like an arrow shot from a giant bow. It took him a few minutes to breathe normally, and then flying at superspeed felt easy and he could hear the reindeer chatting over the radio.

'Lift-off successful!' said Dasher. 'Nice work, everybody!'

'Space door opening!' said the voice of Father Christmas.

For one scary split second Jake was sure the sleigh was about to crash into the artificial sky of planet Yule-1, but a trap door suddenly opened in front of them and they zoomed through it.

'**WE'RE in SPACE!**' gasped Percy. 'Are you OK, Jake?'

'Yes, I'm OK,' said Jake. 'Isn't it beautiful?' He had watched a lot of documentaries about space travel, and explored the solar system on his computer – but this was different. Nothing could have prepared him for the enormous, unending darkness, the flashes of ghostly light when they passed stars, or the clouds of glittering space dust. He knew he would never forget the amazing experience of flying through the rings of Saturn, or the very strange fact that Saturn smelt of bad eggs.

'**Meteor shower ahead!**' cried Dasher. 'Lucy, put up the shield!'

'Yes, skipper!'

The shield was invisible – the shower of meteors

bounced off it without hitting the sleigh.

Jake had no idea how long the dreamlike journey lasted before he heard FC in his headphones. **'GRAVITY ADJUSTER ON!'**

The sleigh dodged around something that looked like a vast lump of grey rock, and Jake only just had time to realise it was the moon – his own moon that he had seen so many times from his bedroom window on earth – before they broke through the atmosphere with a violent **BUMP** that he felt in every cell of his body.

'Oh, help!' cried Percy beside him. 'I forgot about that bit!'

It was night-time on this part of the earth. The sleigh flew over villages, towns and cities, all twinkling with lights and suddenly freezing cold – Jake saw snow on the ground, and remembered that it was Christmas Eve.

Next Christmas Eve, which meant that they were in the future. If he flew over his own house, would he be there, lying in bed? It was too confusing to think about and he pushed the thought into the back of his mind.

They were now flying low enough to see Christmas trees, and windows filled with coloured lights. And then Dasher called out:

'SOOT UP AHEAD – THAT'S GOT TO BE KRAMPUS!'

The soot looked like a thick black cloud, and it was moving very fast. Something awful was happening down on the ground – wherever Krampus and his stolen sleigh passed, all the Christmas lights disappeared. There were no more trees or cribs or street decorations. And then a ball of fire shot out of the cloud of soot, missing the sleigh by inches and spinning them violently off course.

The next few minutes were the most terrifying of Jake's life. The sleigh tossed and bucked and seemed about to crash to the ground, he heard Percy screaming beside him, and then the sleigh was steady again.

'FASTER!' shouted Father Christmas. 'We've got to stop them meeting up with their wicked contact!'

'I think my stomach got left behind!' squeaked Fred.

'We're getting close,' said Jake.

They followed the black cloud along an empty road that Jake recognised from his many trips to his gran's house. He was about to call out that they were coming to the big concrete model of Thomas the Tank Engine – but the words died in his throat.

Thomas wasn't beside the road now. He was in the middle of it – a jaunty blue engine with a smiling face – and they all heard the angry shouts of Krampus and Nerkins.

'GET OUT OF THE WAY!' yelled Krampus. 'You don't scare *me* – you stupid, human-loving engine!'

There was a loud explosion, which covered Thomas with black soot.

'FASTER!' shouted Father Christmas. 'We've got to catch them before they find their friend!'

Across the sheds and fields of the museum, they heard a chorus of steam whistles.

'This is the one!' Jake cried out, wriggling in his reindeer harness so that he could point at the big shed where they had seen the bad engine. 'In here!'

The stolen sleigh crashed through the roof of the

shed, and for one sickening moment it looked as if the History Makers were too late.

But then they heard a furious scream from Krampus. **'WHAT?** What do you mean, you've *turned good*?'

'Sadie was right!' gasped Jake. 'The bad engine isn't bad any more!'

Down on the ground he saw the stolen sleigh burst out of the wall of the shed – followed by a huge black engine.

'**Ho-ho-ho!**' roared Father Christmas. 'After them, my brave reindeer! Hunt them down, my good steam engines!'

The noise of steam whistles was so loud it made Jake's ears ring, and then he saw something truly amazing. Every single engine in the museum – even the very small engine that pulled the tiny train for visitors – was chasing Krampus and Nerkins across the fields. It didn't seem to matter that there were no tracks. The good engines smashed into garages and ploughed up the earth in people's back gardens.

'**HELP!**' screamed Krampus.
'**STOPPIT!**' screamed Nerkins.

Clouds of steam rose up around FC's sleigh as he led the engines in the chase along the empty motorway – Jake saw two policemen getting out of their car with a look of astonishment on their faces. When they saw FC's sleigh, they jumped back in the car, turned on the siren and joined the chase.

The sleigh was flying near the ground, where they could see the terrible unChristmassing that was happening wherever Krampus's shadow fell – the lights going out in all the houses, the decorations disappearing.

'The Turbo-cake is wearing off,' Jake gasped. 'I'm losing strength!'

'Me too!' cried Percy. 'But we've got to keep going!'

Now there was a big church ahead of them, with a life-sized Nativity scene outside it. Jake caught a glimpse of the figures around the empty crib – Mary and Joseph, shepherds, a cow, a donkey – so beautifully Christmassy that Jake hated to think of Krampus destroying it.

'FASTER!' roared FC.

And then – just as they were catching up with the criminals – Fred let out a squeal of terror and started spinning so fast that all the reindeer harness got tangled up and the sleigh gave a great shudder.

'Fred, stop spinning!' shouted Jake.

'HELP!' cried Percy, and to Jake's horror, his friend's harness snapped and he shot off the sleigh.

The small reindeer zoomed right over the heads of Krampus and Nerkins, smashed into the life-sized Nativity scene, and landed on his bottom in the empty crib that was waiting for the baby Jesus.

TWELVE
We Wish You a Merry Christmas

Jake was never exactly sure what happened next, but suddenly everything was different.

FC's sleigh drifted gently to the ground, the steam engines put on their brakes.

The police siren stopped.

The stolen sleigh flipped over and shook Krampus and Nerkins out.

Percy said, 'Ouch, this manger is *hot!*'

He scrambled out and a golden light poured from the manger, so bright and strong that it lit up the countryside for miles.

Father Christmas knelt down on the frosty earth.

The reindeer knelt.

The two policemen knelt.

The steam engines bowed their funnels.

Jake dropped to his knees and his exhaustion melted away into a feeling of happiness and peace.

Even Krampus and Nerkins knelt before the light, though they were very sulky and cross.

'We did it!' said Father Christmas.

He stood up, the light in the manger faded – and it was Christmas again.

One of the policemen asked, 'Is there anything we can do, sir?'

'No thank you, officer,' said FC. 'Happy Christmas!' Lights twinkled in every window, the church bells rang, the soot around Krampus and Nerkins changed to glitter. The steam engines tooted their whistles in a chorus of 'We Wish You a Merry Christmas', and the happiness spread out across the whole world.

* * *

'Are you OK, Perce?' Jake ran to his reindeer friend.

'I'm GREAT!' said Percy, beaming all over his furry face. 'Though my bottom's a bit singed!'

Somehow, a feast had appeared, right in the middle of the empty motorway. There were sweet haycakes for the reindeer, the good engines ate top-quality coal and there was a big Christmas tea party for the humans. Though Jake didn't see how it happened, they had been joined by his parents and Sadie.

'Well done, Jake!' Mum hugged him. 'We're so proud of you – and so glad you're out of danger!'

'That was really fun!' said Sadie happily. 'One minute we were fast asleep, and the next minute we were flying here in a big puff of magic smoke!'

The parents of Percy and Fred were here, too. Mrs Prancer hugged Percy with her front legs. 'We got quite a shock when we suddenly found ourselves flying – you've been very brave, and I'm the proudest reindeer mum in the universe!'

'**My pooh-cake!**' cried Mrs Dancer, covering Fred's face with big, smacking kisses. 'Oh, you must be dreadfully hungry!'

'Yes I am,' said Fred with his mouth full. 'I might need to stay at home just *eating* for a few days.'

'**JOLLY WELL DONE, EVERYONE!**' said Wing Commander Dasher. He shook Jake's hand. 'Jake, I never thought a human could fly so brilliantly! Percy,' – he shook Percy's hoof – 'there's a place in the Jambusters waiting for you when you grow up!'

'**Oh, CRUMBS!**' Percy's black eyes shone.

'And Fred . . .' Dasher was chuckling. 'Maybe after a few more lessons . . .'

'Don't worry about me,' said Fred. 'I don't think I'll ever be Jambuster-material. I'd much rather make tinned moss.'

'What about the criminals, FC?' asked Lucy Blitzen. 'Are you sending them to prison?'

Krampus and Nerkins didn't look scary now, just rather small and grubby.

'You certainly deserve to go to prison,' FC told them cheerfully. 'But I was very impressed by Sadie's work with the bad engine – so I've decided to let her invite you to a *real* tea party!'

'Serves you right,' said Jake, laughing. 'She's really bossy.'

'OK,' growled Krampus.

'I don't mind,' said Nerkins. 'She is a bit bossy, but her pretend cakes are *fantastic* and I can't wait to try a real one!'

There was a special, separate picnic tea spread out on the road, just as Sadie and Belinda had designed it – except that now it was real.

'Come and sit down,' said Sadie. 'I knew you wanted to turn good! Now you have to say please and thank you.'

'I think that engine wants to join us,' said Belinda, smiling at the formerly bad black steam engine.

Everyone stood aside to let the engine join the tea party. Sadie patted him kindly and Krampus and Nerkins sat down next to him.

'The engine says it's nicer being good,' Sadie told

them. 'He says he's made lots of new friends. Wouldn't you like some new friends?'

Both criminals mumbled, 'Yes!' And Krampus cried, **'YUM!'** when Sadie gave him a big plate of trifle.

Belinda gave Nerkins a slice of haycake that was decorated with chomp-nuts. 'I expect you're sorry for being naughty now.'

'Yes,' said Nerkins.

'Sorry, FC,' said Krampus. 'Maybe humans aren't so bad! I don't want to put coal in their shoes any more.'

'I'll find you both proper jobs, and a nice little house,' said FC. 'If you promise to behave!'

'OK,' said Krampus.

'I promise,' said Nerkins.

The empty stretch of motorway was now filled with an enormous – and very unusual – tea party of reindeer, humans, former monsters and steam engines.

Father Christmas sat down beside the Trubshaws and the Prancers. 'I'd like to thank you all for saving next Christmas.'

'Don't mention it,' said Dad. 'What's happened to the traffic?'

'There won't be any traffic,' said FC. 'I've stopped time for this party, and it was easier than it's ever been, thanks to my wonderful new computer system!'

'Oh, it wasn't too complicated,' said Dad modestly. 'I enjoyed designing it.'

'It's so efficient now,' FC went on, 'that I can spin time around at double speed. And that means I can send you humans home.'

'Home?' The sound of the word made Jake suddenly homesick for the normal human world. This trip to earth had made him realise how much he had missed the feel of his own planet and the smell of its air.

But then he remembered going home would mean saying goodbye to Percy.

Sadie and Belinda started to cry.

Jake and Percy looked at each other and Percy's eyes filled with tears.

'Goodbye, Perce,' said Jake shakily. 'Thanks for everything, mate – and good luck with your flying!'

'Goodbye, Jake!' said Percy. 'I'll never forget you!'

The human and the reindeer hugged each other.

'Don't be too sad,' said FC, his voice very kind. 'You two live on different planets but you're closer than you think – nothing can spoil a friendship like yours. And you will see each other again. I'm hoping you can all come back to Yule-1 for a few days every holiday – Jake, you have quite a talent for teaching my reindeer to fly.'

'That's true,' said Percy. 'I couldn't have done anything without your fabulous flying lessons!'

Jake was so happy that he couldn't speak – he would see Percy again, and he would fly again. It was the best Christmas present ever.

'Can I come, too?' asked Sadie.

'Of course!' said FC. 'It'll take more than one tea party to keep Krampus and Nerkins in line. And though I'm going to wipe your parents' memories in the short term, I'll need them too – Mr Trubshaw to maintain my computer system, and Mrs Trubshaw to carry on her splendid work with the Reindeer Library.'

'That's nice,' said Mum, smiling at Mrs Prancer. 'I was just getting started with that library, and Poffle Glen is such a lovely place to stay.'

The Trubshaws and the Prancers hugged each

other, all smiling now that they knew it wasn't really goodbye.

'Cheer up, Jake!' said Wing Commander Dasher. 'I'll be delivering your presents next Christmas. You won't see me, but if you're thinking of leaving a reindeer snack beside your stocking, I really like chocolate ginger biscuits.'

'OK,' said Jake.

'Cheer up, Belinda!' Lucy Blitzen, from the Janiacs, took off her pale-blue velvet bonnet and gave it to the little reindeer, who beamed with happiness and pride.

'Your parents won't remember any of this when you get home,' FC told Jake and Sadie. 'It'll be too complicated for human grown-ups to understand, so they'll be surprised all over again when I summon them back. But you two will remember – and as a reward for the help you've given, you'll *always* have lovely Christmases.'

Time gave another jump, the air had the soft warmth of a summer night, and Jake found himself lying in bed inside the holiday cottage. Just as he wondered sleepily if it had all been a dream, he heard a voice calling outside – '*Happy Christmas to all, and to all a good night!*'

* * *

The rest of the Trubshaws' summer holiday was wonderful. Mum and Dad said it was the best holiday they had ever had – though they did wonder why their children kept talking about Christmas, and why Sadie had so many pretend tea parties.

When the next Christmas came round, Jake carefully put a chocolate ginger biscuit, as requested by Dasher, beside his stocking. In the morning the biscuit had gone and he found something very special in its place.

'Where did that scrap of paper come from?' asked Mum. 'I'm sure it wasn't there last night!'

The scrap of paper had a small hoofprint on it, and some wonky writing –

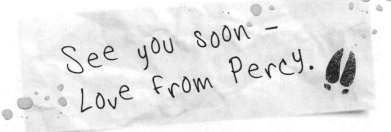

See you soon –
Love from Percy.

THE END

Afterword and Acknowledgements

The names of FC's reindeer are
taken from a very famous poem,
A Visit From St Nicholas
by Clement Clarke Moore.

The Bressingham Steam Museum really
exists – but there are no bad engines.

I'd like to thank all the people who helped me while
I was writing this book – especially Marion Lloyd,
everybody at Faber and Faber and my family.

And whatever time of year it is,

HAPPY CHRISTMAS!